The Hide and Seekers

A novel for children

by Adoni Patrikios

D1444471

All contents of this book are works of fiction and should not be seen as representing or construing any real people, places or events.

Additionally, although hide and seek is fun, you should only do it in appropriate places and, if an adult asks you to show yourself, you really must, even if you've found a really good spot and you don't want to.

Chapter 1.

Sandy held her breath and didn't move a muscle. She knew there was one spot in the room where if you looked up to your left you could see one of her shoes. But her shoe was dark, the wardrobe she was hiding on top of was dark, she was in shadow.

The mansion they were playing in was filled with beautiful old furniture, all of it so large it made you think it had originally been built for giants. Now empty, except for visitors intrigued about the past, it was a sprawling playground for their hide and seek game.

As long as she didn't move there would be no reason her shoe would catch the eye.

Whoever was in the room, however, was being slow and thorough. They must have had a sense that she was in there.

She tried to listen to the breathing but it was unclear. It could be Tom, Uncle Jack, or Tabitha but probably not Isaac.

Isaac had told her where he'd planned to hide on the condition she didn't try to find him there or tell anyone because he was so excited it was such a good spot. He was right, there was no way they'd find him before her. She was resigned to being second today.

Isaac had found a recess up the wide Edwardian chimney in the main reception room. He planned to climb up and lean back so that you couldn't see him even if you thought to look up the chimney.

Uncle Jack might think of it, maybe, but since he was a total germaphobe it was unlikely he'd get too deep into it, though he might send Tom up there.

The creaking of the floorboards was now right below her and she felt the wardrobe doors open. It was a large solid wooden wardrobe with a chest in the main section and a secret compartment behind the shelves. She'd contemplated the secret compartment but that was a little too obvious. If you knew what you were looking for it was obvious it was there. The shelves were not as deep as the main section, something had to be behind it.

That's why climbing on top of the wardrobe had been a clever idea. There was a lip on the top, running all of the way around it, meaning it had a natural concealment. And it was so tall that the height discrepancy between the top of the inside and the top of the outside was not at all obvious. It was just a shame that she couldn't quite fit.

She heard whoever was searching step into the cupboard and then the click of the secret compartment opening and some shuffling. There was a snort she recognised. It was definitely Tom down below. He'd thought he'd cracked it, reached in to grab whoever he thought was hiding in there, and been disappointed when his hands had grasped empty air.

She heard him step out of the closet and make another noise. It was almost a 'hmmm' but not quite. She knew her brother well. He was trying to imagine what he would have done if he had found the secret compartment and then decided not to use it. Where would he have hidden?

Tom was a habitual climber whereas as she was not, so that worked in Sandy's favour, but it was not a huge leap for him to think she might climb. Her time was limited now, she knew, but she still lay still, breathing only quietly, not moving at all.

Tom started moving back across the room to the window.

'I know you're in here.' he said to the room in general. 'I can feel it.'

Sandy almost poked her head over the lip to take a peek and see how close she was to being found when she got a lucky break.

From downstairs came the unmistakable sound of Isaac sneezing. It was always the same, three sneezes all in a row, shot out in rapid-fire. He could maybe hold one in but he'd never manage to hold in all three.

Tom was out the door like a shot. She heard him running downstairs. She could hear Uncle Jack and Tabitha too. They were coordinating. Triangulating.

She sat up cross-legged and waited. Downstairs Tom and Tabby would have worked out Isaac was in the reception room. Uncle Jack would work out he was up the chimney and with Tom there it would be no problem to find a volunteer to go up and verify. Isaac was toast. Given his location, maybe even burnt toast.

A minute or so later she heard the call. 'Come out, come out, wherever you are.'

Sandy clapped three times as loudly as she could, spacing the claps out by a second.

Footsteps on the stairs told her they'd heard her and a few seconds later they burst into the room, Tom first, laughing when he saw how close he'd been. Tabby was next, her red hair adorned with a few cobwebs, then Isaac, sooty and dirty with a cheeky grin.

Finally, Uncle Jack came in. 'Good spot Sandy my dear.' He said in his lilting tones. He lifted his arms to her and she hopped down into them and onto the floor.

'How long Jack?'

'Oh, let me check.' He pulled out his watch. 'Exactly one hour and three minutes give or take a few minutes and seconds.'

'Not bad.' replied Sandy. 'It's a big house after all. Who was first?'

'Me,' said Tom. 'I was in the greenhouse. I thought it would be a good double bluff. Who hides in a glass house in hide and seek, I thought. But I guess Uncle Jack thinks the same way.'

'Not your fault Tommo.' said Jack, getting down on one knee. 'I happened to walk past and noticed the windows were steamier on the inside than they had been earlier. Your breath gave you away, and everyone has to breathe.'

'Should have thought of that!' groaned Tom.

'Don't beat yourself up Tom.' said Tabitha. 'It took you longer to find the room I was in, but when Dad walked in he found me straight away.'

'It's a bit of a cheat my dear.' said Uncle Jack kindly. 'They say dads have a special sixth sense for their daughters. Make sure they're not in trouble. Your mum would still be looking for you now I assure you. Come on you guys, let's go and find Mrs Dewberry and thank her for letting us use this house for our game. And if I'm not mistaken she might just have a few scones for us to enjoy too.'

They followed him out on to the landing and down the stairs to the guest house where Mrs Dewberry lived. It has been another great day out for the Hide and Seekers.

Chapter 2.

Sandy and Tom were enjoying their long summer. It wasn't filled with activities or camps. There was no real outings or entertainments but they were enjoying it because both their parents were there for a change.

Their dad, Dr Samuel Myer-Stone, was an archaeologist who disappeared for months on end in the south American Andes or in the deserts of the middle east. He'd been to China, Egypt, Somalia, Tibet, India, even Japan, organising digs and helping to uncover the past. But this summer he was home, and as he had promised, the closest he'd come to digging up any old relics was when he'd helped sort out the old boxes of clothing from the attic.

Sandy couldn't believe some of the clothes her parents had worn when they'd been younger. Dad almost only ever wore khaki these days, whether he was working in the field, at the university or out on a date with mum. It was hard to imagine him in the black leather jacket covered in badges, or that he would ever have walked around in denim jeans, denim shirt and denim jacket.

Mum's wardrobe, by contrast, was very similar to how she dressed now, the only difference being that all the jackets had oddly large shoulder pads. Sandy had enjoyed putting them on and walking around in them, but she couldn't imagine ever wearing them properly, or why anyone would need such big shoulders. They looked doubly silly on her since the jacket was also too big, but Mum had assured her they'd looked silly back then too, only everyone was wearing them so you didn't realise.

As an artist, Sandy's mum, Maggie, had a very distinctive style which had not changed much over the years and that applied to the art she made as much as how she looked. Sandy was ten, and could not remember her mother ever really looking different, whether she was painting dreamily in her studio, meeting buyers at a gallery opening or going to watch a film with her at the cinema.

They'd seen three movies together that summer; a musical, a comedy and a silly action film. Mum had cried at all three, and so had Dad. Her parents could be a little embarrassing it was true, but she was loving having them around every day.

Tom felt the same. He was nine, and every bit a nine-year-old boy, always jumping around, climbing things, rumbling with his friends and being messy and noisy, but he was loving the time with his parents. He'd even spent an afternoon just sitting about in Dad's study reading with him, although Dad had been reading a journal about some Persian ruins whereas Tom had been reading about The Flaming Obsidian, a superhero who was indestructible and could breathe fire.

*

Samuel and Maggie Myer-Stone were enjoying their summer too. It was a welcome change of pace to be able to all be together. Maggie was taking inspiration from her kids and their romps and as much as she was ever working or not, this was as close to not working as she had been since the kids had been walking.

She'd stolen away a few days here and then to work on some of her pieces and had got up early to look at them and finesse them in the early light. The art was half inside and half on the canvasses. It was safe, it wasn't going anywhere. She felt oddly comfortable leaving it there, knowing there were better things to be not-working on; her family!

It wasn't just having her kids there though; it was having Sam too. He was so often out of the country that any extended time with him at home was an opportunity she knew was too good to miss.

Sam loved hanging around with his family too, and the summer had been a wonder. At first, when the dig he'd planned had fallen through, he'd been a bit panicked and had worried about how they would fill the time. Now, he realised, there was more to do than they could ever hope to do in the holiday. Between movies and walks, picnics and parks, beaches and bushland, museums and restaurants, they couldn't possibly do everything that everyone wanted to do.

His favourite part though was the planning. They'd talk at dinner and after dinner over board games. They'd plan as they brushed their teeth and said good night. They'd discuss it some more over breakfast and as they did some chores or gardening as the day began. And eventually, as they sat down for morning tea, still no closer to a decision and decided to just hang at home for the day, or maybe walk down to the high street for some nice bread, that was when he was happiest because he knew then that there was a whole world out there but they were happiest right there, together.

It was the perfect long summer. All of the Myer-Stone family were happy.

And then the phone rang...

Chapter 3.

Uncle Jack was not actually Sandy and Tom's uncle by blood but he was still their closest family.

He had been married to their mum's sister, Lisa, who'd died giving birth to their cousin Tabby. Sandy had only been one, Tom hadn't even been born. The four cousins only knew of Lisa from pictures and stories but there was a huge hole where she should have been in their lives and they all knew the hole well.

They knew Lisa was kind and gentle, funny and smart. They knew she loved her children and all her family more than anything in the world. They knew nothing could have made her happier than knowing all of them were happy.

Uncle Jack came from a different state and did not have any family locally. He had been welcomed into, and welcomed, Lisa's happily. After she passed there was never a question of that being broken. Once you were in you were never out again as far as the Myer-Stones were concerned.

Tom loved seeing his dad and uncle Jack together. It was like one of those clips where two unlikely animals became the best of friends like an iguana and a lemur or a cat and a goldfish.

Dad was so serious, wise and direct, even though his eyes were always smiling.

Jack by contrast very rarely said anything serious or anything that could be understood on the surface.

If you asked him for the salt he'd say 'good idea' and pour it on his own food and keep repeating that until his food was covered in too much salt. Then he'd eat it, telling everyone about how perfectly seasoned it was, how the balance of saltiness was just right for that specific dish, how it was just what he wanted, even as his face told you he was eating the saltiest thing in the world.

Dad would pass you the salt and tell you a fact about salt like how the dead sea or brine lakes come to be so salty, or how Roman soldiers were paid in salt and that it used to be a commodity like gold.

But no one, no one in the world, found Uncle Jack funnier than Dad, and when the kids at the table were done with torturing Uncle Jack by making him add more salt to his food it would be Dad in hysterics as Jack swallowed down every bite, crying with laughter as Jack did his bits.

One time Mum had told the kids that Jack had a tongue injury and couldn't taste anything which is why he could do his routine and when they didn't believe her she'd proved it by getting them to put all sorts of ingredients into his food like chilli sauce in his yoghurt, vinegar on his spaghetti and even strawberry jam in his tacos.

He'd eaten it all without seeming to notice and they'd thought Mum was right, only for him to take them aside after the third time they'd spiked his food to tell them that he actually could taste perfectly well, but had told their mum he couldn't as a joke many years ago and had never revealed the truth.

He asked them to not reveal that they knew that he could taste anything and a couple of weeks later when he'd been helping Dad in the attic he'd pretended to fall down the ladder with a massive thump. Mum had found him and helped him up and he refused the hospital but that night at dinner he acted out the whole meal as if he was a man tasting food for the first time in years.

He claimed the bump on his head must have cured it and told Mum that her Brussels sprouts were a symphony of bitterness and the buttery mashed potatoes were like clouds crying in his mouth.

Mum was flummoxed, Dad was in hysterics as usual and the kids were either laughing riotously at uncle Jack's over the top descriptions or at Mum's amazement at seeing Jack firstly recovering his taste but then lavishing praise on her standard meat and two veg dinner.

The best was yet to come however at desert when *he tried ice cream for the first time* and claimed it wasn't to his taste. Ice cream of all things! He said it was missing something, then poured half a cellar of salt on it, tested it, declared it perfect and ate the whole thing.

Dad had literally cried with laughter, bent over on the table. All the kids had too and by that point Mum was so confused that Sandy had told her the truth, that Jack had always been able to taste food and had been tricking her for years.

That was when the best part of the meal happened. Mum picked up her bowl of ice cream and poured it over Jack's head. After that, they always referred to it as 'that meal' and Mum refused to have either salt or pepper on the table when Jack was there.

Having fun and keeping everyone happy was something Jack took seriously. It was why he'd invented the Hide and Seekers.

Chapter 4.

Dad picked up the phone, said a few words and then quickly took it into his office, closing the door behind him.

Without doing so consciously Sandy and Tom moved towards their mother, and stood either side of her, staring at the door and waiting for it to move. Maggie put an arm around their shoulders and hugged them.

They all knew it was a work call, otherwise why would Dad have gone into his office. And they knew it was a serious work call because he hadn't told whoever it was that he was on holiday. That meant it was someone important.

After what seemed an age the door opened and Samuel stood staring at them. His look said it all. He was excited but tense and distant. He wanted to go straight away, that was clear, but was forcing himself to stay still, forcing himself to confront his family.

Maggie spoke first. 'I know you haven't said yes yet, but you will.'

'I might not.' he replied. 'I said I'd talk to you first.'

'None of us will stop you.' Maggie continued. If it's got this far we'll miss you but support you.'

'I know.' said Samuel.

It was only then that his children realised he looked sad. Excited but sad. Tom found it confusing and wanted to hug his dad or be hugged by him, he wasn't sure which. Sandy was happy. Seeing her dad like that told her everything she needed to know about what was happening. He really, truly didn't want to go. It was breaking his heart to leave them all. But when you're one of the leaders in your field it comes with a certain responsibility.

There had been a pause so Sandy chimed in. 'Well don't keep us in suspense, tell us about your next adventure.'

Samuel moved into the room fully now and sat in the padded armchair beside his office door. 'A bit of a rescue mission this one. Do you remember Alan Cowell, I worked with him in Sumatra about 4 years ago. Anyhow they're in

Uzbekistan digging up a Bactrian settlement and they've had some problems with the local government. Al was out of the country at the time but his entire dig team has been placed under house arrest after a skirmish with the locals there. Seems like a bit of dispute over some remains and the area they're digging may be *Achaemenid* or may be *Medesian* which is what they're trying to discern, so that's not helped...

'I know that's a lot but the short version is I know the current ambassador there, he used to be in Jordan, a nice guy named Saeed. So Alan was hoping I could go help out with some of the politics and then maybe supervise one of the two sites to speed things up and resolve the question of what they're looking at because if it is *Medesian* it's likely we'll need to tell the Iranians pretty quickly and share the site or there'll be a much bigger incident and well... as he put it; If there's one person in the world who gets on with the Uzbeks and the Iranians *and* can speed up a dig *and* can discern the difference between a post or pre-annexation village... I mean there's really only me.'

'So...' started Maggie. 'You're going to Uzbekistan?'

'If it's okay with you guys, yes.'

'Where's Uzbekistan?' asked Tom 'It sounds made up.' He was still upset that his dad was going to be leaving.

Samuel moved over to Tom and got down on his knees in front of him, placing a hand on his arm. 'Oh no, not made up, it's an ancient place, right in the middle of Eurasia. That region was the centre of the world once, seeded by Persians and invaded by Mongols and Turks, Russia even, a huge treasure trove. It's filled with treasures there. The Ulugh Beg observatory is 500 years old and one of the grandest astronomical constructions of antiquity.'

Samuel started getting excited. He stopped being a father and started being an excited archaeologist. 'And then there's the golden ring, a desert now but filled with fortresses, the proper name even means *Fifty Fortresses*, although no one has found them all, all so eroded they look like outcrops of rock they're so old. It's really a fascinating plac...'

Samuel didn't have a chance to finish. Tom burst into tears and ran from the room. Samuel got up and went to follow but was stopped by Maggie. 'Don't.' She said. 'I'll go in a minute.'

'I think it sounds exciting.' said Sandy. 'But when are you leaving? Have we got one more night together?'

'We do.' said Samuel. 'If I say yes, that is. But just the one, I'd be gone before you get up tomorrow.'

'Not if I stay up all night or set an alarm for, say, four in the morning.'

'Sure. But maybe, if I do say yes, instead we could just have a nice night together and I would kiss you good night and know that you'd have a good night sleep before I leave?'

'Maybe.' said Sandy truculently. 'Although what I do with my alarm clock is my business.'

'More importantly than tomorrow,' said Maggie, 'is how long, when will you be back?'

'I might miss a couple of weeks of the next semester I would think. It should be okay, Ryan can cover.'

Ryan was Samuel's teaching assistant at the University. Maggie did some quick arithmetic on her fingers. 'So that's seven, almost eight weeks?'

'If I say yes!' said Samuel again.

'You have to go!' said Sandy. 'No one else in the world could!'

'I agree,' said Maggie, 'It's a no brainer.'

Sam shrugged. 'Still, two out of three isn't enough. Let me talk to Tommo first.'

'No,' said Maggie, 'you're going regardless, and he knows it, it's not fair to pretend he has the power to stop you, you just go and start getting your stuff together. The rest of us will prepare a special meal for you. I know what camp food does to your tummy, let's give you a good foundation.'

She left to find Tom and to start planning their last family meal of the summer. As she left the room, she turned her head and called to her husband. 'Oh, and you'd better let Jack know too. He'll want souvenirs!'

Chapter 5.

Tommy didn't talk to anyone the day his dad left although Maggie and Sandy did at least see some evidence that he'd at least used the bathroom. Maggie told Sandy to leave her brother alone for the day and instead set things up to get him out of his funk the following morning.

Her approach was three-fold. At eight the following morning she started cooking his favourite breakfast of bacon and eggs with toast and ketchup. She did it noisily then popped it on a plate, put the plate on a tray and swept into his bedroom and left it on his bed as he stirred awake.

Maggie understood the value of a good breakfast and sat at the kitchen table with Sandy to eat their food, drink coffee and juice and read the morning papers.

Sure enough prong two kicked off without a hitch. Tom came into the kitchen to ask if there was any juice, bacon always made him thirsty, and when he did his mum reminded him that there was no juice in the bedroom and that he'd have to bring his breakfast in and sit at the table with them.

Tom trudged off to his room, somewhat sulkily sat down, and helped himself to apple juice, eating silently and not looking at his mum or sister.

Maggie pulled the funnies out of the paper and pushed them over to him. She carried on reading the day's news. Tommy couldn't resist the cartoons and then moved on to the basic crossword.

They sat there enjoying the morning until unexpectedly the doorbell rang. Prong three had arrived.

'Who's that?' asked Sandy.

'I don't know.' said Maggie, shrugging. 'Mailman maybe? Tom, can you go and check?'

Tommy got up and left the room. When he got to the door he could not see the vague outline of a person on the other side of the opaque glass, which was unusual. He opened the door a little and peeked out but there was no one there so he opened it fully.

On the front step, on its own, was a large cardboard box big enough to fit a washing machine inside. There was something unusual about it, but he couldn't tell what.

'Who is it?' his mum called from the kitchen.

'No one.' Tom called back. 'It's a box. Someone left it here.'

'Bring it in then.' Maggie replied.

'I don't know if I can, I think it's too big.'

'Is it heavy?'

'I don't know.' said Tommy, walking up to the box and putting his hand on it. He saw the label now, handwritten, not printed. It said:

For the immediate and sole attention of Thomas Myer-Stone

Not to be opened by anyone else, at all, ever.

Contents are fragile and must be handled with care.

Do not, under any circumstances, set fire to this box.

'Check?' his mum called out.

'It's for me.' Tommy called back. 'I think maybe Dad sent me something?' he wasn't sure because he didn't recognise the handwriting.

His hand was still on the box and he gave it a shake. The box wobbled easily, but the bottom didn't budge, it was like it had something very heavy in it, but not something that completely filled the box. He bent down and grabbed a corner trying to pick the box up but whilst the corner rose a small way, the box itself remained anchored to the floor. It was definitely too heavy for him to lift.

Maggie and Sandy turned up on their doorstep. 'What is it?' they asked.

'I don't know.' said Tom, giving it another shake. 'I can't lift it, can you help me get it inside?'

'Why not just open it here?' asked Sandy. 'Then you'll know where to move it to.'

It started to dawn on Tommy that there was something very unusual about this box and that his sister and mother knew exactly what was in it, but he was more than happy to play along.

He turned back to the box. The top of it was just around his eye level but he could reach over and grab the flap on the top.

He got his fingers underneath it and gave it a good yank. Immediately 5 purple balloons floated out on strings and stopped, bobbing a metre or so above the box.

Tommy smiled, then leant forwards to see what the balloons were tied to. He grabbed the edge of the box and got on his tiptoes to look in. It was dark inside and he was just focusing his eyes to understand what it was he was seeing when the thing he was seeing moved, rushing up towards him. Tom jumped back quickly and tripped backwards, landing on his behind just as his cousin Tabby leapt up inside the box, holding the balloon strings and screaming 'SURPRISE' before folding over in a fit of giggles.

From out of nowhere Uncle Jack and Isaac appeared smiling happily and there was the flash of a camera as Tom sat on the floor, his mouth open in a surprised gape.

'Delivery for Master Myer-Stone!' laughed uncle Jack. 'It's your favourite uncle and cousins.'

'My only cousins and uncle.' laughed Tommy. 'Why were you in the box Tabby?'

'I won the rock paper scissor competition we had in the car.' she said. 'Isaac and Dad were desperate to get in it too, we couldn't decide otherwise. Your face was soooo funny.'

'Need helping getting out?' Jack asked his daughter.

'No chance.' she said. 'Take these and stand back.'

She handed the balloons to Tommy who was back on his feet and then ducked down inside the box. The box started shaking as she threw her weight against one of the walls of it and it toppled over. Tabby rolled out.

'Come on Tom, let's take this box to your room and make a cubby.

Tom grabbed the edge of the box and the two of them dragged it inside, the balloons trailing behind them.

Jack gave Maggie and Sandy kisses on the cheek and started sniffing the air. 'Is that the unmistakable smell of Myer-Stone bacon and eggs?'

'You hungry Jack?' asked Maggie.

'Even if I wasn't I'd still want a serve, but yes, I'm starving. I haven't eaten for like... half an hour.' He patted his belly.

'How about you Isaac? You want some food too?'

'No' said Isaac. 'I ate half an hour ago, with Dad!'

'Come in anyway, everyone. Come one.'

The four of them went inside and closed the door behind them.

Chapter 6.

'It's a once in a lifetime opportunity.' said Jack, pushing his plate away and then pulling it back towards him to pick little bits of bacon off of. 'I was just lucky my friend told me about it and was happy to play along.'

'And you're sure it's not dangerous?' asked Maggie.

'No, not at all. There's a couple of weeks before the crew come on board to start the refurb, which is the demolition. He's just sitting there with a booth and some security cameras around the fences with his finger on a panic button just in case. It's just a hotel on supports in a massive empty... pool.'

'Empty pool!' said Sandy. 'Must be a big pool.'

Jack pointed to everyone at the table as he spoke. 'I don't think any of you really appreciate how big a full-on cruise ship is. They're like... massive. Really massive. And that's just the outside, remember they go down even further than the water line. It'll blow your mind. But imagine...'

Jack drew a large rectangle in the juice on the bottom of his plate with his finger.

'This is a massive swimming pool next to the sea. And this is the door.' Jack grabbed a string of crunchy egg white and laid it across the end. 'When the doors are opened it's just a... a... a man-made harbour, but you can close the doors if you want but why would you. The important thing is it's big enough to fit a ship.' He moved the egg to the side.

Jack stood up, grabbed a piece of bacon from the frying pan and brought it back, chewing on it until it was the right size for his demonstration. 'So this is the ship, the Radiant Queen is what she's called, and in it comes.'

He placed the bacon ship on the plate and sailed it into the rectangle he had marked out. 'In it goes and once it's in you close the door and then it still goes up and down with the tides but it's protected from waves and swell so it's safe to work around. Then you go in underneath and you put these big supports in the right place, so it doesn't tip, but actually, the bottom is pretty flat anyhow. Anyway, they go in then you seal the door properly...' he pushed the piece of egg firmly into place, 'and then you pump all the water out slowly. The ship sinks and sinks until it's resting on its supports and then the water is gone and you have it in dry dock. People can walk around the bottom, put in scaffolding, cranes, whatever you like, and it won't move around.'

He looked at the four kids sitting at the table and smiled. 'There's just one danger of course.'

'What?' asked Tommy.

'Every now and then, even after the ships been sitting there for a while a…. massive hand can come down out of the sky pick up the cruise ship and eat it.'

In a flash, the bacon was in Jack's mouth. 'But that rarely, if ever, happens.'

'And we won't get in trouble?' asked Sandy. 'For being there when we shouldn't. Normally we have permission.'

'That is true.' said Jack. 'This is a little different from our normal adventures because the ship's owners definitely do not know we will be there and would definitely say we cannot be.

But, if we use a little imagination… Andy, my friend, works for the security company that protects it, he's basically like the teachers, right? He's looking after the ship for its parents.

'And you know how teachers are, they won't let you leave school without a permission ship from your parents, will they? No slip, no excursion, that's the rule.

'So it's the same with Andy. He's the teacher, the ship is his student he has to look after, the owners are the parents.

'But! Maggie, have you ever had to sign a permission slip for an incursion?'

'What's an incursion?' asked Isaac.

'It's when people visit your school. Like when those guys came in to tell us about road safety.' said Tabbi, 'Or when the people come in to do Yoga and that sort of thing.'

'Exactly. Excursions are one thing, incursions are quite another. Would Andy be allowed to take the cruise ship for a trip up the coast? Certainly not. But letting a few people on? Of course he can. And he'll be working tomorrow himself as it happens, so it's not like anyone else would even know...' Jack let the words hang.

'So you're sure it's safe. And we won't get in any trouble?' asked Maggie.

'We? Will I have a triple Myer-Stone contingent?' asked Uncle Jack.

'Oh, please Mum, please come.' said Sandy.

'Yes, Auntie Maggie, it would be so good if you were there.' said Isaac.

Maggie smiled and half nodded. 'I can't think of a reason why not, I always love hearing about your adventures and so rarely join in. I'd love to experience this one. I'm quite curious about a cruise ship too.' Maggie had never been on one, nor wanted to go on one, until Jack's breakfast based description.

'I think that's settled then.' said Jack. 'The Hide and Seekers are going to the Radiant Queen tomorrow. And would you like a cup of tea Mags? I need to make one, that breakfast, great as it was, needs a little washing down.

Jack stood up and went to the kettle but Maggie didn't answer. She was watching the four kids at the table who had erupted with delighted chatter.

Chapter 7.

Uncle Jack was an unusual germaphobe in as much as he was the sort of germaphobe who was often very dirty.

He explained it simply enough. When his mind was on other things, he said, he couldn't care less about the trillions of bacteria, fungal cells, viruses and other micro-organisms that covered his body.

On the other hand, if he allowed his mind to contemplate the things he had touched that day, the other things that had touched it before him, the ambient temperatures and humidity and the breeding ground that was therefore surely slowly taking over his body, well, if he did think about that he would be aghast and have no choice but to flee to the nearest restroom and wash away with all his might.

Even contemplating a simple doorknob could be enough.

And then, of course, he would have the danger of being confronted by thoughts about the things he might be touching in the bathroom, and what else might have touched them.

He might even begin to think about the air, about the particles, and how the air was always touching everything equally and that he was constantly under assault.

Thoughts like that could ruin Uncle Jack's day, which is why he really tried very hard to not have thoughts like that. Much easier than to keep his mind busy with other things, with activities and jokes and nonsense.

This did make uncle Jack by far the best uncle one could hope for, and a pretty great dad too, but it had its downsides.

The obvious one, of course, was that inevitably a panic would happen occasionally and anyone with him would find themselves either inside the bathroom with him, or waiting by the door as he frantically washed every bit of exposed skin he could.

The less obvious one was that Jack was always turned on and full of beans and ideas. It was his mechanism for dealing with a world out to get him after all. And that was as true at six in the evening as he entertained you after dinner as it was at six in the morning when he came to pick you up to go on a hide and seek adventure.

Jack knocked on the door seven times, waited about 3 seconds and then started again, not stopping until a bleary-eyed Maggie opened it.

Behind Jack stood Tabby and Isaac, both looking much like Maggie felt but with the extra exhaustion of having spent forty-five minutes asleep in a car with their dad before the sun had come up.

'Come in' croaked Maggie, shocked at what she sounded like. 'Does my voice sound funny?' she asked as she shepherded the three of them into the kitchen.

'You sound a bit like a frog.' said Isaac quietly, sitting at the kitchen table and putting his head on his hands.

Jack gave her a sideways look. 'Are you okay Mags? You sound sick.'

'I'm not sure. I only just woke up, let me get a cup of tea in me.' She went to the kettle, filled it and put it on the stove, returning to the table where the two kids were lying down on it and Jack was sitting bolt upright like the little drummer boy. 'Did we agree to start at… I don't know what time it is. Early? Did we agree to start early?'

'Well we agreed to start in the morning and it's a three and a bit hour drive to get there so if you work backwards from that…' Jack trailed off. 'You really don't look that well. Are you sure you shouldn't head back to bed?'

'I think I'm okay, I just might need to wake up a li…' Maggie did not manage to finish her sentence. Instead, her body was caught up in trying to eject something from itself. First came a couple of large sneezes. Maggie grabbed the back of a chair to steady herself and then started coughing almost immediately, a deep chesty cough that made her face go red.

The kettle started whistling so Jack went to turn the heat off then took his sister-in-law by the shoulder. 'My dear,' he said calmly, leading her out of the room, 'you are no more fit to be up and about than I am to be down and away, let's get you into bed and you should stay there for the day. Consider it a stroke of luck if you like, I'm here anyway and my car takes five, so we'll save on some petrol and get you well again in one fell swoop. Come on now.'

Maggie didn't protest, although she did sneeze again, and sloped off to her bedroom and back under the covers.

Jack opened the doors to Sandy and Tom's bedrooms and saw them both fast asleep, then went back to the kitchen where his children were similarly unconscious.

'Did you know kids' he started, despite knowing they would not hear him, 'that the sense of smell does not turn off even when you're asleep and is very much underrated as a means of rousing oneself. Who needs an alarm clock, when you can have an alarm breakfast instead.'

He started rooting through the cupboards, finding ingredients and building a plan in his mind.

Twenty minutes later Sandy and Tom wandered into the room, bleary-eyed but drawn by the incredible smell of omelettes with onions, capsicum, mushrooms and cheese, waiting on the table for them along with buttered toast and freshly squeezed orange juice.

Tabby and Isaac were already eating and Jack was tidying up but turned to then. 'Morning kids, right on time. Get that breakfast in you. There's been a change of plan, Mum's sick, but I'm not, so get a nice breakfast in you and get ready, we're leaving in exactly...' he looked at his watch, ' twenty-three minutes.'

'Morning.' said Sandy, sipping her juice. 'How long have you been here?' she asked Tabby.

'I'm not sure.' said Tabby, between mouthfuls of omelette. 'I think we saw your mum but it was dark. Dad made us sleep in our clothes last night and carried us into the car. It was so cool, we just like woke up and we were here.'

'Yeah,' said Isaac. 'You know how he is on hide and seek days.'

Chapter 8.

Mitchell Terry was not the most confident he had been in his long and relatively successful criminal career.

Successful was very much a relative term. He'd never been caught or gone to prison, but he was permanently broke and always looking for the next job.

He'd followed a pretty tried and trusted route. He'd started with stealing bags and mugging people as a young man, always being careful to travel to do either so no local police ever got used to him or his methodology.

Next, he'd stepped it up to burglary, shops at first and later houses, although he'd always found stealing things, as opposed to money, somewhat pointless since once you'd stolen it you had to sell it. Selling stuff was very much a job he was not good at, and by the time he'd been haggled down to a price, the buyers would accept it never seemed worth the hassle.

'Mitch,' they'd say, 'The problem is I just can't sell it. Who wants a second hand, stolen, used TV these days? Who wants thirty pairs of Nike trainers in assorted sizes?'

Mitch barely, and rarely, broke even. Not worth the risk he concluded. But you had to give it to Mitchell, he was not a common career criminal. He was introspective. He thought about himself, he thought about what he was doing and he thought about how he could do it better. He had aspirations.

Aspirations, and a brother that he felt beholden to look after even though - much like the time he'd accidentally stolen 4 boxes of fake gold necklaces, recommended retailers price $9.95 - he was little more than a weight around his neck pulling him down.

Blake Terry was not the sharpest knife in the drawer. He was like a butter knife in a world that was an old piece of rubbery steak. He was a career criminal too, but not like Mitchell was.

Mitchell planned and schemed, analysed and improved himself. Blake woke up each morning and wondered what the day would bring.

Mitchell negotiated and fought to get the best possible deals he could, whilst acknowledging his inadequacies as a negotiator. Blake liked avocados.

It was not a natural fit but Mitchell made it work. Job by job he tried to up the ante and come out on top dragging Blake with him as muscle or numbers, sometimes lookout or driver. Blake wasn't completely useless, not at all, a good crew needed a certain dynamic, it needed different skill sets, it needed star players and water carriers.

But no matter how much he planned and schemed Mitchell never quite found that big score and he was beginning to carry that with him like a weight on his chest when he started new jobs. Even jobs like this which in theory were easy, where they had an inside man, where the risks were low and the gains were high, where even Blake has a useful role to play. His confidence was mounting.

It had all started when he'd met Kenny in a pub which was not frequented by the nicest fellas but which had the advantage at least of being quiet. Kenny and Mitchell had got to talking as men do about sport and the state of the world.

As they had a few more beers Kenny revealed he was a bit down on his luck himself having been put out of work recently. Mitchell had asked what he'd done and discovered he'd worked on a cruise ship, below decks, as a mechanic.

They'd talked about cruises, about people that went on cruises. Mitchell led the conversation well. He'd never really thought about crimes on the high seas but he had a question that maybe Kenny could answer.

On a cruise ship out in the ocean, how much liquid or real value was there? If you combined all the crew and all the passengers and made them empty their pockets how much money would there be just floating on the ocean. It was a question that you could not ask in many places but in this pub, it was a fairly normal and reasonable question.

Kenny did not know. He estimated the passenger count and Mitchell tried to establish how much money they would have on them when Kenny explained it wasn't quite like that. Cruises tended to be all-inclusive or have their own currencies. They were not necessarily cash rich.

Just as Mitchell's interest started to wane Kenny Deans thought of something. The safe. A lot of people, he explained, took very expensive things with them, or bought them on the cruise. Jewellery and cash too, it's just they all got locked away.

That had been enough. Mitchell had started thinking. He knew a good man to work on safes, Robby 'Knuckles' Newman, not a nickname he got for fighting but because he had tiny hands: hands all the better for the delicate art of safe work.

The plan had grown from that seed and now here they were in a van, on their way to the dry dock to put part one of the plan into action. It was simple really, clever when you thought about it.

The safe wasn't really a safe, it was a safe room filled with security boxes. Any passenger who needed one could access the room, but they could only access the boxes with a key that they were given when they first filled the box.

Breaking into all the boxes mid-cruise was too hard, but if you could easily open them all then a passenger with the right master key or the right set of keys could simply ask for privacy and empty every box. Mitchell could be that passenger. They rig the entire room, he throws a watch in there when he gets on board and mid-cruise he could just walk in and empty it all out.

He could then stow it, or drop it over the side for collection or he could jump over the side himself for collection if he was feeling brave.

They had the access they needed if they bought one ticket.

They had the means they needed if they had a way to open the boxes.

And they had the place to do it if someone could simply take them to a ship when no one was looking at it, when it wasn't at sea and when it was accessible and safe and empty; in dry dock.

This was everything that Mitchell's career had prepared him for. It was the long game, the smart game. It was safes and conning, robbery and fencing. He might not be able to sell TVs, shoes or mobile phones with any real aplomb but he knew good buyers for gold, silver and diamonds. And if there was any cash all the better.

They just had to get inside the barely guarded 'Radiant Queen' make their way to the safe room and let Knuckles do the rest. It didn't matter if it was weeks later, months later or even years, Mitchell felt certain the day would come when his ship came in. Literally.

He wasn't the most confident he'd been no, the plan was complex and long, with multiple stages and many unknowns. But he was certainly the most excited he'd been for a long time.

Without intending to he reached over and slapped his brother on the back, smiling. Knuckles, Kenny, Mitchell and Blake. They might, he thought, just might pull this off.

Chapter 9.

There were many hours of driving to the dry dock where the Radiant Queen was being kept. The car was crammed with kids who needed frequent toilet breaks as well as Jack's insatiable desire for coffee and car snacks.

They drove through emerald hills dotted with the moving clouds of sheep, past villages that came and went, no more than a shop and a post box, a memory even as they slowed down to enter them.

Jack was in his normal bright spirits and sung much of the way, either aloud to the kids, or, if they were otherwise engaged, to the songs on the radio, to himself, sometimes singing his own song whilst the radio played another and the children sang a third again.

Lunch came up over the horizon as they broached a hill that looked down on the dockyards.

'Look there kids.' said Jack, pointing out the front. He pulled the car to the side of a road in a gravel soft shoulder that abutted a woolly field that had evidence of its former inhabitants, if not the sheep themselves.

'Come,' said Jack, climbing out the car, and opening the boot. He arrived on the passenger side with a cooler-box and gestured the kids to follow him out of the car. Turning, he climbed over the fence and marched off across the field.

The kids, not expecting this, rattled out of the car to follow him and as the last door slammed behind them Jack locked the cars via the remote without even looking back.

They followed him as he stomped halfway across the greed field which sat on top of the hill that overlooked the dry dock. Jack joined with a stony path that cut across the field and headed down it towards a low wizened tree under which the bedrock was exposed.

Jack pulled a picnic rug out of the cooler box and started setting up for lunch as the kids joined him, all except Tom who had been staring at his feet and realised that the path, cleared of grass as it was, was none the less very much covered in sheep poo to a startling degree.

Tom enjoyed maths and had some skill at it. He had used the length of his shoes, which he knew to be 20 centimetres long heel to tip, to estimate the width of the cleared path at around 30 centimetres. Using some basic geometry, therefore, if he measured his shoe again along the path equally and made a square, then marked it out and added just a little, he could then mark out an area of around one thousand square centimetres on the path.

If he counted every poo in that area he could then multiply it by ten and work out the number of poos per square metre. He could then go further, and multiply it again to estimate the total number of sheep poos in the field.

Jack had taken out a variety of containers and set them up, with Isaac, Yabby and Sandy sitting around him, looking at what he produced. There were sandwiches in three boxes marked egg, cheese and peanut butter, as well as another container of chopped up fruit, a jar of olives, a sleeve of crackers, three bananas attached at the stem, a sandwich bag of dried fruit and a very large pickle in a container all on its own.

'Dig in!' said Jack. 'Better to eat now than hide hungry. But no one touch the pickle! That's mine.'

'As if we would!' laughed Tabby, no one likes your pickles except for you.

'Not yet, but once you get the taste for them you'll see, you'll be begging me for my pickles and my secret recipe.'

'Doubt it.' said Sandy, also laughing. 'I remember I tried one once. It tasted like the worst salt and vinegar crisps I'd ever had squished inside a wet slug!'

The children all giggled whilst Jack pretended to be offended.

'Hey!' he snapped. 'Who told you my recipe. Anyhow it won't do you any good, you don't know where to get the good slugs from anyway!'

That set off more titters before Isaac picked up the sandwich box marked *Cheese* and discovered it only had jam sandwiches in it. Sandy and Tabby both picked up the remaining containers and found the peanut butter ones also had Jam sandwiches in them, and the egg ones the same.

'Why did you label them like that Uncle Jack?' asked Sandy.

'Ah. Well, you see, I had planned on making egg sandwiches, and cheese sandwiches and peanut butter sandwiches too. But when I went to make them I discovered that I didn't have cheese or eggs or peanut butter, only jam and pickles and a little bit of ham that smelled funny.

'*Well*' I thought to myself, '*that's no good really but the kids won't mind*, I mean, kids love jam sandwiches, especially when they're on lovely soft white bread with a generous serve of soft creamy butter.

'But then I realised your mum was going to be here and I thought she wouldn't approve of us all having jam sandwiches for lunch, even if they did come with lashings of beautiful creamy butter, as I mentioned before.

'But!' Jack spread his arms very wide. 'I then realised that your mother does not eat sandwiches. She never does unless there's nothing else to eat because she says the bread makes her feel bloated. So very cleverly I packed some olives and some rye crackers which I knew would draw her attention, and then I labelled the boxes up as if they were healthier sandwiches since if she didn't know they were all jam sandwiches, and if she never actually tasted one, and you kids kept quiet about it, we could get away with it.

'Quite an ingenious plan if you ask me. Although ... I now have a jar of olives that have come for a field trip but will be heading back to the fridge feeling like they've failed us.'

Sandy smiled then bit into a jam sandwich. It was divine. The break was soft and white, the butter creamy with just a hint of salt and the jam an explosion of flavours, tart strawberry with a silky texture. 'They're great uncle Jack.' she said. 'I don't know how you do it, but you make the best jam sandwiches.'

'It's because he buys so many jams.' said Isaac. 'Every market, every stall we pass, every jam on offer he'll buy one and if it's no good we throw it away, or not really, we give it to the Jennings next door.'

'They weren't that keen on it at first.' said Tabby, 'But once they got used to it they didn't mind. Free jam with just a teaspoon's worth missing from them, and they get a review too.'

'Too tart, too lumpy...' said Jack. 'You get the idea. Talking of too lumpy, where is that brother of yours Sandy. Ah, there he is!'

Tom was standing twenty metres away next to the path, holding a pile of black things in his hands.

'Tom?' asked Jack. 'What are you holding?'

'One hundred and eighteen sheep poos,' said Tom, smiling. 'How big would you say this field is?'

Everyone on the picnic blanket burst into laughter and Jack reached into the cooler again, this time bringing out a container of hand sanitiser and some wipes

He stood up and walked to his nephew. 'I don't know how I knew I would need these Tommy, but somehow, this morning, I just knew I did.'

Chapter 10.

The drive to the dockyards was quick. Jack's friend Andy was waiting for them at the gate. He was a large man, bearded and stooped, like the butler of a decrepit mansion where standards had significantly dropped, but he had the twinkle in his eyes that the kids all recognised from Jack himself, a sparkle of fun and kindness. He gurned a variety of funny faces at them through the windows as they drove past and met them in the car park, embracing Jack in a heartfelt hug and introducing himself to each of the children directly.

The dockyard was a massive flat area like a razed industrial park with the obvious exception of the massive cruise ship rising out of the middle of it surrounded by gantries, cranes and other large devices.

The kids asked if they could go look at the sea, and the kids ran off together to the edge, near the cliffs that looked out over a hundred meters of craggy rocks and eventually to the ocean.

They laughed and jumped around, working the car cramps out of their legs and followed the edge of the compound till they came to the giant dry dock doors that separated the channel in the rocks from the huge pit that the boat sat in.

Two huge doors were guarding the enclosure which looked like an emptied-out swimming pool stretching from deep below sea level all the way up to the cliffs they were standing on.

The cruise ship itself was huge, but not just huge. They were used to huge cruise ships, that was a category they all had in their minds. But the category was, of course, only ever above the waves. From where they stood, staring from one corner of the sunken pit and looking diagonally across at the Radiant Queen, it was truly immense. It was a marvel, rising as far down from them as it did up, a colossus of metal and determination.

'Geez.' sighed Isaac. 'I can't believe how big it is. We could get lost in there for days.'

'It's mad.' agreed Sandy. 'I think I understand why it doesn't sink. It's a boat, of course it doesn't sink. But when you see it like this, you think like... *Wow! That's going to sink.*' she raised her voice dramatically to make her point.

The others agreed and they continued walking along the edge of the pit, staring at the boat as they approached the first of the machinery laying around it.

A whistle from ahead let them know Jack wanted them and they hurried up, jogging, jostling and eventually racing to him where he was waiting, alone, at the bottom of a staircase.

The staircase was freestanding and four storeys high, made of rugged red painted metal. On the third floor, a platform emerged and struck off across the void as a bridge, supported by struts that went all the way down to the base of the dry dock, scaffolded together in an intricate interplay of scaffolding and concrete.

'We're ready.' said Jack. 'I have the all-clear from Andy and he's briefed me on safety protocol, in short, this platform and these stairs are the only way off other than jumping into the water and he very strongly suggested we do not try and do that at the moment.'

'Why not?' asked Tabby, laughing before realising for herself. 'Oh. Squelch!'

Jack nodded deeply. 'Exactly. So remember where this gangway is as it's the only way home. And as I assumed, no work has started yet so everything is perfectly safe and there is battery power at least but we all need one of these.' He held out his hand which contained five nondescript grey security passes. 'All the doors are secured but these passes will open any door on the ship. The lifts will not work, no lifts.

'The only thing is, and Andy really asked me to reiterate this, there are places on this ship where it is not safe for adults, let alone children. He mentioned the engine rooms for example, but also the main lobby is five stories tall, so you'll need to use your common sense. If it looks dangerous stay away, and if it is dangerous don't do it, but I assume I don't need to say this. Right?'

All the kids nodded. Tommo was already on the bottom step.

'Take a card then and walking only, carefully, sensibly, let's go.'

He handed out the cards and followed the kids who ran up the stairs as if they were not there, feeling his old legs catch up with him before he made it to the gangway platform. By the time he reached it the kids were halfway across and still jogging, and were on the ship waiting patiently long before he was halfway across and trying assertively not to look down.

Jack didn't stop when he reached them and ploughed on through the nearest set of double doors, leading them down a short corridor and then through a service door straight into the main lobby of the cruise ship.

It was an incredible sight. Somewhere between palatial opulence and a Jurassic jungle with huge planter boxes throughout, each filled with soaring ferns and gargantuan bromeliads, all sitting atop plush red velvet carpets. Every edging was gilt-edged. Every sconce was decoratively opulent.

High above them, forming the ceiling covering the lobby, was a skylight that completely covered the area, high above the balconies, open corridors and sculptures that filled the vertical space up to there.

In the middle of the lobby was a circular reception counter and Jack led then there, whistling appreciatively as he brushed his finger over the marble slab of its counter.

'I don't think we should have any further ado. Kids, first-round stay on this level. I will count to a hundred. Find you soon!'

Jack leapt over the counter and got down low.

'One. Two...'

The kids looked at each other and then the surroundings.

'Three. Four...'

They giggled nervously and smiled, making faces at each other, trying to form quick, silent partnerships.

'Five. Six...'

Without saying a word they split up and fled, Tabby and Sandy heading behind the back of the counter and to the doors to the central plaza, Isaac heading off alone through the service door they'd entered in, Tommo circling the counter once before disappearing, in his quietest footsteps, towards the casino.

Chapter 11.

Andy was sitting in his cabin reading the newspaper. It was an old-fashioned thing to do, he knew that. A thing from the past that was longer really done. To get the paper he had to drive out of his way to a newsagent, get out the car and pay with actual cash for it. To get actual cash he often had to stop on the way to the newsagent, another detour, just to collect it from an ATM.

But, to Andy's mind, if you were going to spend a day in a booth, monitoring screens, a gate and a large dry dock whilst nothing else was going on there, you really couldn't beat a newspaper, a good stack of sandwiches and a working kettle.

He read the whole thing over the course of the day, every piece of news about the country, the world, business, sport, the funnies, the games, everything. It made him feel informed because he knew when he read news on the internet he just chose stories he liked the look of. The truth was that as much as he read he retained almost nothing except the horoscopes, which he faithfully relayed to his wife in the evenings.

She was a Scorpio, and sceptical, and it was their little game to take the day she'd had and see how well it aligned to the horoscope he presented to her. Normally it didn't and he tried to convince her that it did. Very occasionally it matched almost perfectly and she tried to convince him that it didn't at all.

He was just reviewing the classified sections, wondering if he was someone who would benefit from a gutter cleaning service at top prices, when something caught his eye. That something was a van coming down the road towards him. It was a particularly noteworthy van for one very simple reason, no one ever drove down the road he wasn't expecting and he was not expecting anyone, not for a couple of weeks.

Very occasionally some travellers would get their GPS in a muddle and take the wrong turn whilst heading for Chamber's Beach, but they were normally in campervans, kombi vans or cars that looked like they'd circled Australia four or five times and had the kangaroo dents to prove it. This was not like that, it was a work van, a hi-top white van with tinted windows. There was something else odd about it too, but he couldn't quite work out what, either through the window or on the monitors filming its arrival.

The van pulled up at his office and stopped. Normally at that point, the vehicle's window would roll down and a conversation would happen but in this case, it didn't. It just sat there, the engine running. Andy had a bad feeling in his stomach but he also had a job to do. He got up and walked to the door of his hut, opening it and standing tall. The windows were so tinted he couldn't see anything at all inside.

He pulled his pants up slightly, ambled forwards and made a gesture with his hand, a rotating gesture that meant clearly, roll down your window, even if almost no one rolled down their windows any more.

Like an iceberg or a very heavy book of poetry, the van just sat there.

Andy walked over to the window, and, as politely as he

could, he leant forwards and tried to peer through the inky darkness of the window.

Somewhere at the back of Andy's mind some brain bits were firing off and putting together a picture of what he had seen. There was a van, and there was something wrong with it, but he couldn't work out what. And just like in the spot the difference games he did in his paper every day, the answer was obvious. Something was missing that should have been there. Something that really should have been there. It was a number plate.

And there was only one reason a tinted-windowed van would remove its number plates, and that was to avoid any identification if it was caught on camera.

It was the van equivalent of wearing a balaclava, obscuring the key distinguishing feature.

All of this connected in Andy's head with a pleasant ping, in the way that solving a little puzzle can.

And that ping was joined but a very loud donk, provided by a wooden club hitting the back of his head, held in the hands of a strong and large man in a balaclava who had quietly snuck around the back of the van for that purpose.

That man was Blake Terry. And he didn't read newspapers. Ever. But he did quickly pick up Andy and carry him back into the booth where Robbie 'Knuckles' Newman secured him with skilfully tied ropes, leaving him lying bound up in the corner on his side.

Kenny Deans got out the van by the passenger side, also wearing a balaclava, and walked into the hut, opening the gate to let the van through. He hit the close gate button and took up residence in the hut, turning off the security cameras and checking the man was still out cold. He leaned back in the chair, took off his balaclava and pulled out his old company-issued ID badge and the walkie talkie that connected with the rest of the crew.

He relaxed and smiled to himself. He even had a paper to read, he loved the paper.

Of course, had Kenny gone any further with the rest of his crew he would have been able to point out the one thing that no one should have seen. The second car. Jack's car. As it was the van continued down to the gantry without a second thought, unloaded and came back to park in the parking lot.

Kenny, meanwhile, was enjoying the sports section.

Chapter 12.

Tommo had originally looked at the casino and thought it was perfect. There were multiple machines, tables and bars with nooks and hidey-holes, not to mention the various over the top decorations. There was a lifelike replica of a polar bear, spear-wielding Eskimo, dog sled, dog pack and igloo in the centre of the room for Pete's sake! It wasn't called The Polar Lounge for nothing.

The room was quite literally stuffed with hiding places.

However, as he quickly came to realise, they were all very shallow. As he lay in his chosen spot he realised why. This was a casino where people gambled with real money or with chips that were basically the same. If it was filled with really good places to hide people, things or what you were up to, the casino wouldn't like that.

Some proof of that was that he was slowly counting more security cameras on the ceilings and walls than he had ever seen anywhere.

Every table offered a place to crouch under, but anyone on all fours would see you instantly from almost anywhere else in the casino. The decorations only even gave you cover from one angle. Even the bars were raised - on legs – and the machines were spaced out enough that whilst you could creep between them, you would also be seen from one side of their grid set up or another.

As Tommo had processed all of this he'd run out of time. He had seen the other's scatter and knew there was a one in three chance Jack would be coming his way first so he'd panicked, climbed on top of the bar counter and then up on to the top of the bar itself and was lying as flat as he could, his eyes on the entrance door, ready to make himself flat and invisible.

He was a little annoyed at himself, his first instinct was always to climb and get high and Jack knew that, it was like his tell. On the other hand, the top of the bar section was relatively wide and he was relatively sure that if he moved to the exact centre of it Jack wouldn't be able to see him from ground level.

*

Of course, Jack was an expert seeker and knew the sound of his kids, as well as his niece and nephew. Tommo's idea of walking, even creeping, quietly was a distinct crunching and foot sliding that was like a laser beacon for his chosen direction, especially combined with the signature loop of the counter, designed to confuse.

He followed the sound of those steps into the casino and started narrating, as he sometimes did, especially when he was feeling confident.

'Tommo, Tommo, Tommo.' he said, shaking his head. 'A casino. Really? What were you thinking? I know you're nine but still, you must realise that a casino is a terrible place to hide.'

Jack got down on his knees and crawled forwards until he was confident he'd seen under every table.

'They don't lose people in casino's you must know that. Lose a person lose money, that's a fact! So you're not under the tables, that's good. And I don't suppose you'd be dumb enough to hide inside an igloo would you?"

Jack walked to the arctic scene and peered inside the igloo and then, dramatically, inside the mouths of first the polar bear and then each of the husky dogs individually.

He moved on towards the machines, surveying the room as he did. 'Those plants are all nice and big, but not hide an entire person big. The balloon arch is a joke, the craps table would only make sense if I was two foot tall...' he got to the compound of machines and walked down two of their sides, ruling out any wedging action.

'But you know Tom, the thing is, you're not really a wedger are you. Nor a crawler. You're a panicker, still, even after all those games.' Jack took a stool from a colourful machine and pulled it over to the bar. 'And what do people do when they panic? They revert to type. And what's you're type?' Jack climbed on to the stool and then on to the bar counter. 'They do what comes most naturally. Which in your case is, of course, to seek shelter up high. Which is why I know... based on the scuff marks on the side of this bar, that you are up on top of it. Are you going to come out or you going to make me climb up there?'

There was a silence, not even a breath.

'Fine.' said Jack, reaching over and holding on to the top of the bar. 'Tom Tom Tom, I found you.' Jack leant forwards and pulled himself up so his eyes were above the level of the top of the bar, staring at the angry face of a nine-year-old boy.

Tom screamed a scream of delight and agony then sat up and accepted his uncle's help to get down safely.

Chapter 13.

Jack found his daughter and niece cunningly hidden in the central plaza's dining area. They were lodged within the large cursive lettering of a burger bar called Sandy's Grill that formed both the outskirts of its seating area and a hugely exuberant sign. Sandy was in the G curled around, with Tabby sinuously entwined within the initial S.

The three of them followed Jack as he led back where they'd come from and towards the outer deck they'd initially walked through into the ship.

The kids knew not to help him but were allowed to go with him, and were keeping as quiet as they could, knowing Jack was a big advocate of seeking by ear, listening out for the creaks and groans that were not just the non-living structures.

'Isaac is adventurous.' Jack opined out loud. 'He likes to explore, so he wouldn't have found anything too close, and I definitely heard him come out this way. But! He also knows that I know he's adventurous. So would he deliberately go somewhere close and try and psych me out? Or is his ploy to make me doubt myself and do something I think he wouldn't do because he thinks I'll think...'

Sandy put her hand on Jack's arm. 'Uncle Jack. Isaac spoke about toilet paper for half the journey here. I don't think he's thinking like that.'

'You're right!' said Jack. He turned his back to the side railing on the walkway that went all the way around the ship and looked both ways. There was no way to choose which way to go first, both directions would circumnavigate the ship but, with the limited time of the count in his head, Isaac would have prioritised getting around a corner which meant heading towards the front of the ship.

He walked slowly in that direction, listening as well as he could given the rising rush of the wind and the occasional seabird startling in the distance.

Because of the nature of the deck, there were mercifully few doorways on the level, most transit being from within the ship to this floor but as he started to turn curve to the rear he saw this didn't hold true entirely. There were a couple of service doors and then a very large opening through to the deck bar which was opposite the elaborate swimming pool, now empty, and water features.

There was a number of hot tubs around the main pool, which featured a sunken bar and underwater stools so you could enjoy refreshments without even getting out the water. To the far left an extreme slope of fibreglass shot up in the air, connected to some water spouts, all festooned with pictures of waves and stereotypical surf lingo. A surfing machine of some sort.

A lap swimming pool, just two lanes across, went across the deck from port to starboard with a bridge over it that led to the tower that strutted up from the front of the ship, a zig-zag of metal stairs and platforms that gave access, at three different heights, to water slides that looped around the structure and into exit pools to the right, left and centre.

This ship, to Jack's mind, looked fun. And he knew that Isaac would think so too, that structure would be completely irresistible to his offspring. He quickly checked the door to the main bar area but could see in any case it was closed from the inside with a gate that sealed it off. The door did not open and there was no key pass, in any case, so he headed around the pool, listening and looking, carefully, into every planter box and foghorn, while knowing where he was ultimately headed.

Jack climbed the stairs to the slides and went straight to the top, pushing himself into the tube. Without the waterjet it was not slippery and he had to scootch his way along on his bottom, a gruelling endeavour.

He came out at the bottom disappointed, waved at the remaining kids and launched himself into the exit pool of the middle slide, crawling up it and emerging on the platform a couple of minutes later sweating slightly.

The was only one slide left, the smallest, so he walked down a flight of stairs and crawled headfirst into it.

Sandy, Tom and Tabby watched the exit of the slide from across the deck with anticipation and whooped with delight when they saw first the dusty brown head of Isaac coming round the last bend of the slide and then the larger person bustling him out and head butting him off the end of the slide.

Isaac quickly ran away, leaping over the side of the exit pool, dropping over the side of the main pool and running around its curved sides until he came to the bar, and took a seat, red-faced, out of breath, but smiling. The other kids jumped down and joined him and waited on the stool as Jack walked towards them, looking a little red and sweaty himself, but otherwise full of the joys of life.

'Okay!' he shouted, as he lowered himself into the pool and started walking across it. 'Hands in the air. Who enjoyed that game!'

Eight hands went up, two from each kid.

'And keep your hands up if you need a little rest and a drink.'

The hands stayed up, so Jack reached into his bag and handed around water bottles and some of his home-dried apple rings, sticking a few on his fingers as he did so.

He sat at the remaining seat of the bar and looked out at the sky. 'You know given how I am not that into being on boats I don't mind this.'

Sandy slapped his arm. 'You mean you don't feel seasick!'

'Exactly!' snapped back Jack. 'It's just a weirdly shaped hotel with amazing facilities in the middle of nowhere, exactly my sort of thing.'

Tommo laughed and started moving his body side to side, nudging Isaac to join him, the girls following suit. 'You sure it's not moving Uncle Jack? You don't feel it going side.... to... side.'

Jack watched them swaying and despite himself felt his tummy turn just a little. He turned away and looked out at the sky again, getting them out of his eye line. 'I'll have you know I do have my sea legs. They're just a bit rusty.' He was going to on to tell them about his time on a fishing boat in Papua New Guinea, but the giggling and chatting reminded him that he did not need to be the centre of attention, and he enjoyed their babble and the sun on his face.

Chapter 14.

Maggie woke up at the stroke of twelve feeling groggy.

She dragged herself to the bathroom, used the facilities, washed her face, then her neck and eventually decided to go all-in, jumping into the shower and ratcheting it up as hot as it would go.

The steamy jets blasted her body and the water vapours filled her head, eking into her sinuses and slowly dissolving the build-up. She blew her nose in the shower and found, to her surprise, she could almost breathe normally by the time her hair was washed and conditioned.

She turned off the water and stepped into her bathrobe, wrapping a towel around her head and moving to the kitchen, noting that Jack, as always, had cleaned up after himself that morning. She turned on the kettle, poured herself a glass of orange juice and sat at the table whilst she waited for the water to boil.

She felt... good. Surprisingly good. Those hours in bed seemed to have taken her from feeling like death to feeling just a little snotty and blocked up. Whatever virus it was seemed to have passed through her and been shaken off with just the lingering hint of a headache.

She made her tea and found she could smell its bitter tannins easily. The house was calm, the house was quiet. With Samuel overseas she had a rare opportunity to have the whole house to herself, she could do anything she liked.

But, she realised, she actually felt a little lonely. Samuel wasn't just overseas, he was away. And her kids too. And Jack, and her niece and nephew. When she thought about it, everyone she cared about was elsewhere.

She checked her clock and did a quick calculation. It was twenty to one. If she got moved real fast, just got on with it, into her car and away, she could make it to the ship by about four, especially if she didn't stop on the way. And maybe she'd not be able to join in the games, but they could come back slowly together, she could take the girls maybe, they could all stop for dinner. There was bound to be a nice restaurant, or a café, or a decent club near the ocean.

And if there wasn't, there was always fast food and car games.

She didn't think about it any further, she poured her tea into a takeaway cup, quickly dressed in some rumble-ready clothing and grabbed her bag. She had keys, wallet, phone, everything she needed.

As she walked to the car she messaged Jack.

Hey. Feeling better, coming to meet you, call me when you leave if you don't see me there.

She dropped her phone into her bag, got in the car and got the motor started. Bed to on the road in a little over fifty minutes, a good job all round.

What she hadn't noticed in her purposeful haste was that her phone was running rather low on battery. She'd also failed to remember to pack a charger. But she was on the road, she had the radio on and she was off to see her family. She wasn't worried about any of that.

Jack, unfortunately, had not seen this message. He'd not seen that message because the dockyard was in a pretty remote area and was only serviced by the one network, the national one, that he was not a member of. Which meant the phone in his pocket did not beep or buzz or give any real indication of his sister-in-law's impending arrival. In the most basic way possible, it was failing in its purpose to be an information device. A useless brick in his pocket.

When Jack and Lisa had first met it had been one of his many quirks that he did not carry a mobile phone. This was of course in the distant past, an age before time where grown-ups meet and fall in love, but even at that time being phoneless was very unusual, especially a person who could absolutely afford one and was below the age of sixty.

Lisa teased him about it all the time, everyone did, but he was principled and a little stubborn about it and said that he liked to live in the moment and not be dragged away by someone else, somewhere else, who had their own designs on his attentions quite divorced from any appreciation of what he happened to be doing at that moment.

As an attitude it was somewhat charming if you happened to be with him, after all, he was essentially declaring that whilst in your company he was absolutely devoted to that company. Quite by contrast, when you were not with him, it was one of the most unbelievably frustrating things imaginable, since he was absolutely the only person you would know who you could not get in contact with without either calling his house or setting out to find him, the latter being the most common requirement since he was very rarely at home.

This lasted up until Jack and Lisa married, and for a year or so afterwards until a particular incident when Lisa had had a terrible day.

She'd been coming home from work late at night and had not realised she was running low on petrol. She was returning from a client location that she was not familiar with. When she saw the orange petrol light come on she had assumed she'd find a gas station in time, but had not, and had had to pull over on the side of a road, at night.

She waited for five - then ten - minutes for another car but when one didn't come she decided to call for a pick up from roadside assistance.

These were the days before mobile phones doubled as computers and navigation devices so when the operator asked where she needed picking up from she had to admit she had almost no idea beyond twenty-five minutes from the last town heading either north or east, maybe south. She'd agreed to walk back to the previous cross street to find a more accurate location and would call back.

As she walked it started to rain. First a little, then a lot. Then she lost a shoe in a puddle and, in the rainy gloom, could not locate it. She threw the other one away and kept trekking along.

When she came to the crossroad and got a useful location, she discovered her phone was wet and out of operation. With no other choice she just kept walking along the road until, finally, a kind passing driver turned around, picked her up, took her to the previous town, helped her fill up two jerry cans with fuel, drove her back to her car, helped her fill it up and led her down the road to the next petrol station along, made sure she was okay, and secretly paid for her petrol when she wasn't looking.

That man was Alfred Mason, he doesn't have any further place in this story, but a doer of good deeds like that deserves some special praise.

When she got home late Jack was completely relieved to see her having feared the worst and listened to her story whilst feeding her warm soup and dry towels.

'I know exactly where you mean.' he had said. 'It's a lovely road there between Grey Plains and Hester.'

'It's probably nicer by day.' Lisa had said. 'But it would have been nicer still if I could've called you when I needed you there.'

Jack had bought a phone the next day and always had one on him thereafter, sure that he would not be the reason someone could not have his help gain.

Chapter 15.

After eating some apple rings, drinking some water and running around the curved edge of the pool at gravity-defying angles the kids followed Jack as he led them back around the side of the ship and through the door they had initially entered through.

They passed back through the reception area and entered a stairwell, descending down a few stairways and bringing them out through a door on to a long corridor.

'Welcome to first class.' snapped Jack. 'This is where you come if you really want to enjoy your cruise. Every door on this level is a first-class suite. Some have one bedroom, some are two or three, I think one is technically a palace. Your cards will open any of these doors however we do have a small problem.'

'What's the problem?' asked Sandy, smiling. 'This feels like home to me.' She opened the nearest door and pushed her way in, the others following her into the suite. They a large entry lobby with a corridor that ran off it all the way to a window, with rooms coming off each side of the corridor.

The kids all ran off immediately.

'I found a toilet.' shouted Tommo from one side.

'Me too!' shouted Tabby from further inside the suite.

'I think I'm in a wardrobe!' shouted Sandy. 'It's bigger than my bedroom.'

'I'm on a bed.' called Isaac. 'I think it's bigger than my bedroom too.' There was a pause, and then a clear sigh. 'And so soft.' he exhaled.

'There's a kitchen too!'

'I found another bedroom.'

'I found another bathroom.'

'I found that bathroom already. Oh! No, I didn't.'

'The balcony is huge.'

Jack walked along the plush pile carpet, appreciating the give beneath his feet and imagining if he would enjoy it so much if the whole ship was lilting in the waves. He suspected not. He walked past a marble dresser in the corridor that was just there to fill the space and entered the lounge room. A huge fire pit in the centre of the room was circled by plush sunken couches. Entertainment units filled one wall, a bar another. He could certainly get used to this.

He went out on to the balcony and sat in a sun lounger, waiting for the kids as the explored and slowly came to join him, sitting on the remaining sun loungers, the outdoor set or the table nearby, all of which were bolted down quite artfully.

'The problem then.' he said as they settled down their excited chirping. 'This is huge. This suite I mean. We could almost play a game just in here. It's too big if I am honest for a regular seeking game. The floor I mean. But I don't want to limit you and say we can only do this section or that, so I thought we could have a few rules just to make it a bit easier.'

'What are you thinking?' asked Isaac. 'You thinking sardines?'

'I wasn't!' Jack exclaimed, jumping to his feet and beginning to pace excitedly, 'but I am now. Sardines would be a great idea, spread the load a little. I suppose we have our regular candidates for the first hider?'

Tabby and Sandy both shot their hands up.

'Well,' continued Jack, 'You can decide between yourselves. But I still have another rule or we could very much be here till next week, especially with sneaks like you lot. It's a simple rule really, and one that works quite well with Sardines, especially if you choose well initially, whichever of you does so.

'Put simply; if you open a door it stays open. That means you can set up decoys but at least we'll know where not to look. Everyone fine with that?'

All four kids smiled.

'Am I missing anything? Do we need a toilet break? I believe you know where they are if you do.'

No one moved.

'Fine. Tabby, Sandy, who's going first?'

The girls whispered between themselves at a speed and hushedness that precluded the others following what was being said until they turned back to the boys and Tabby piped up. 'It'll be me.'

'Great. We'll just sit here on the deck. You have till a hundred then... fifty each? Maybe Tom, Sandy, Isaac then me? And Go!'

Tabby smiled then fled the room, her footsteps echoing in the background.

'One, two, three...' counted Tommo.

Jack spoke to them all whilst Tommo counted for himself. 'You know how it is with sardines, I might disappear quickly, and I won't be looking for you, so if you do need me just scream and I will break cover, never be worried about ruining the game. And if we see each other in the corridor no teaming up okay? I remember what happened in the tunnels that time. Boys, I'm talking about you.'

The boys grinned sheepishly, Tommo continuing to count.

As he got higher and higher the tension and excitement grew visibly in fidgets and shuffling and he sped up as he hit the nineties. The moment *One Hundred* came out his mouth Tommo was gone and Sandy started counting herself.

She was running out of the balcony and out the suite less than a minute later with Isaac picking up the thread and departing likewise.

Jack stood up and stretched, resting on the railing and looking out at the horizon and counting in his head. The view wasn't spectacular, just the dockyard stretching flatly to the fence but the sun was bright, the air had a snap of crispness to it and best of all the tang of sea salt in the air.

He reached fifty and left to start the seeking.

A few seconds later, had he been still looking out he would have seen a white van with no number plate rolling into view, returning to the car park after unloading. But he was gone, and he did not.

Chapter 16

Tabby fled down the corridors throwing open every other door she passed, leaping from one side of the corridor to another to create both a path of confusion and a breadcrumb of clues.

She doubled back on herself, passed again the suite the rest were hiding in and did the same on the other side, although more spaced out, and, she hoped, more random.

She turned a corner and was out of sight of the room and opened the doors less frequently. In her head, she was at about seventy so she needed to find a spot.

She turned around and decided to count till 8 then take the first open door, which was to her left. It was a suite very similar to the one she had left her family in but smaller. She quickly ran through it doing quick calculus. This one had two bedrooms, but under the bed should be out, as should wardrobes. The balcony was very exposed, the walk-in wardrobe - because every suite apparently needed one – was too small, the lounge room was basic, the sunken floor barely sunken, with no fire pit as a centrepiece.

She realised she'd made a mistake and was heading back towards the entrance when she noticed an alcove to her right. The alcove itself was unremarkable, about the width of a telephone box with a fixed vase and a doily on it. What was interesting about it was that it started at waist height. Ship space was never so luxurious as to be able to just waste space like that to create a recessed table, there had to be something on the other side.

She entered the bedroom behind the wall it appeared in and found the bulkhead projecting out, with a hatch beneath it labelled with an orange emergency sign. She opened the hatch.

Inside was five life jackets, a bag of supplies and ample room for herself to sit in, ample even for all of them probably, it would be a squeeze if Jack wasn't last.

She climbed inside and pulled the hatch closed behind her. It opened towards the door, so she could leave it open a crack without breaking the leave it open rule but from the door, at least on a cursory look, the open hatch would escape attention.

It wasn't a clever hiding spot, but it was a good one statistically. You'd have to roam a lot of rooms to find her.

*

Tommo ran out into the corridor and turned right, noting the open doors ahead of him. He was better friends with Isaac than with Tabby, didn't know her as well as Sandy did either, but Tommo had worked very hard on his hearing. He'd learnt from his cousin Isaac just how valuable listening carefully could be. Whilst Tommo had been counting to a hundred he'd been listening very hard, straining his ears. He'd heard the footsteps disappear, then get louder again before disappearing once more.

Tabby had doubled back on herself to avoid being caught.

The open doors in both directions told him the same but, he also knew that when she had headed out she'd had time on her side whereas when she'd doubled back she had not. One way had fewer doors open. Logically, she would be that way.

He ran down the corridor to his right until he was sure that there were no more open doors.

He turned around and started walking back again, listening acutely. He slowed down his steps, taking long strides and pausing to strain his ears. He heard something, he was sure of it, to his right. The doors here were infrequently spread out which meant only one door could have led to the source of that sound had he indeed heard it. It was clouded too since he could hear stomping in the distance, Sandy on foot and out hunting too.

He entered a smaller suite than the one he had been in and walked straight through to the balcony. The Balcony was clear, as were the drapes and the underneath of the bed. He diligently checked the bathroom, the lounge room, looking not for his cousin but rather for a place where his cousin could feasibly be.

Nothing sprang out on him, if she was here she'd obviously panicked and chosen a poor room, which to be fair was like Tabby. She often left decisions until late and regretted them.

He knew this from buying ice cream with her where she'd umm and err about pear and pannacotta versus chocolate devil surprise before panicking when the person behind in the queue got impatient and ordering lemon, or watermelon or rum and raisin, instantly regretting it.

Tom heard footsteps in the corridor getting louder, Sandy running around, no doubt looking for clues. He moved into the bedroom nearest the door and slipped behind a drape on instinct, peeking out to see if Sandy was coming into this room.

As he did so he noticed the crack of the hatch. When he was sure the coast was clear he opened it up and slipped in beside his cousin.

*

Sandy got very lucky. She had been lost, wondering what to do and knowing she was running low on time having skirted in and out of various suites shallowly when she heard a noise she was very familiar with. It took multiple forms but the essence was the same. A disgusted squeal. An angry grunt. A boyish giggle. Sandy quickly zeroed in on it and the commotion was still going on when she got there.

'He farted!' whispered Tabby, outraged that anyone, let alone her cousin, would do this in a small cupboard with an almost closed door with her.

Tommo was still giggling to himself but moved over, to give his sister some room. The small hatch was packed now, the next person in had to be Isaac or they would have a real problem pulling the hatch closed unless Jack had acquired some significant contortionist skills.

The smell was still overwhelming. In hushed tones, they agreed. They'd keep it open, and all be very quiet so that Tommo could let them know if they heard anything in the distance.

*,

Isaac ran out into the corridor and took a left and ran until he came to the last open door. He was methodical, so he entered that room. It didn't seem to have any good hiding spots in it and as he exited the room he came face to face with his dad.

'Not in there?' asked Jack.

Isaac shook his head.

'Okay. Let's split up, start at an end each, if we meet in the middle we're both idiots.'

Jack gave his son a high five, turned around and ran on down the corridor.

Chapter 17

Mitchell held the map up in front of him and started following it with his finger, trying to trace his way to the secure safe room. The problem was that the map that Kenny had given them was both complete and frustrating.

It was massive for one thing. When they'd been looking at it on the table in their warehouse it had been easy to follow, but standing on the ship it was like trying to make a double bed with a single sheet, pieces of it constantly flopping over or springing where they didn't need to go.

For another thing, the map was two dimensional, with each floor laid out quite neatly, but to chart a route in three dimensions you seemed to need a part of your brain that Mitchell was beginning to think he didn't have, like discovering you were colour blind in the middle of a game of Uno.

He heard stomping behind him then a couple of resounding crashes as his brother and Knuckles dropped their equipment on the deck behind him.

'Which way bro?' asked Blake.

Mitchell scowled, turning the map and holding it higher. 'Just working the best route there, give me one second.

'Don't we just follow the red line?' asked Blake, peering over his shoulder.

'Yes we do.' snapped Mitchell. 'But I am just trying to work out where the red line that Kenny drew on the map actually refers to, it's not as simple as you think.'

Blake looked sad and at his feet. 'Isn't that it?' he asked, pointing down.

Mitchell followed his brother's finger to the floor where a red line ran from the gangway, off to the left and then through a closed door.

Mitchell consulted the map, looked closer and realised that as his brother had correctly surmised the lines on the map were replicated on the ship, Kenny had used the markings designed for passengers to help guide them to the safe room.

Mitchell was unlucky in some ways. He was smart enough to know he was smarter than many people, without being smart enough to recognise the limits to his own intelligence. Given this he quickly surmised that it was easier for someone with so little going on in their head; someone whose brain made the sound of two wind chimes when he thought really hard; someone whose thick-as-sausage fingers saved him the trouble of discovering he couldn't even do maths with a calculator; to see something as obvious as that.

After all, markings on the floor were specifically for people who didn't know where they were or where they were going. That was Blake in nutshell.

'Come on' quipped Mitchell. 'Follow me. We'll follow the red line till it meets the blue line, then a left, and follow the blue line to the end of the corridor and it should be on our left.

Knuckles and Blake picked up their gear and followed as Mitch led them to the first door and opened it with his pass, holding it open for them to carry their bags through before rushing ahead of them with the map so he could be sure to lead the way.

The corridor took them to a wide staircase and down that, past a retail deck and into another stairwell that took them to the blue line.

They followed that past closed doors, bustling along, the clanking of their equipment stark in the silence of the ship's innards.

The blue line took them down another staircase and the décor abruptly changed as they stepped off the blue line and on to the floor with the first-class suites. Everything just looked better here. It went from classy to high class in an instant. From tasty to delicious. From super, all the way to super-duper.

Knuckles whistled. 'Sweet as. This must be where the rich people stay. Can you feel that carpet, that's a thick pile. I feel like I'm walking on money. Piles of money.'

'Wallpaper!' said Blake, reaching out and touching it. 'You can feel the patterns. On a boat. Crazy.'

Mitchell moved to his left and consulted the map. 'That's why we're here.' He said officiously as he did so. 'Money won't come to us so we go to the money. And here.' He stopped outside a double door with the sign *Safe Room* above it on the lintel.

Mitchell folded up his map into a manageable rectangle and shoved it in his back pocket then pulled a card out of his pocket. 'Moment of truth.' He muttered to his colleagues, before tapping it on the pad beside the door.

It beeped.

A Light flashed green.

The pushed and the doors swung open inwards.

Mitchell pulled the walky-talky off his belt and engaged the talk button.

'We're through to location 1. Confirmed we are in. All green at your end? Over.'

There was a pause before Kenny answered indistinctly. He'd just been having a sip of tea, but the men on the ship did not know that. 'Confirmed, all green here. And you don't need to say over.' came the muffled reply.

A split second later the speaker parped up again. 'Over' said Kenny.

'Roger that.' snapped back Mitchell, putting the walkie-talkie back on his belt and entering the safe room.

Chapter 18.

Isaac was a pragmatist and of no little intellect. He realised there was at least a fifty-fifty chance that he was at the wrong end of the hunt. He also realised he was not fond of sardines and with the choice of being the fourth in or the finder, he knew which he preferred, so instead of checking the rooms around him he slowly edged forwards until he could just see his dad disappear into a room.

He lay down on the carpet, as close to the wall as he could, and positioned himself so he could only just see his dad then shuffled backwards until he could only just see the next open door.

After a couple of minutes, he saw his dad enter that room.

He edged backwards against the wall again until he could only just see the next door and he waited. The thick carpet was so incredibly colourful, patterned and eye-catching that he was sure he was well hidden even relatively out in the open and he enjoyed the sensation of it, the give on his bare elbows and knees, the way it was both the ground and also supporting him off the ground.

He pushed his fingers into the fibres and felt like he was stroking the world's largest, firmest bear.

It was hard to judge the passage of time lying there but there came a time when he realised his dad had been in the room a very long time. He wasn't sure that he trusted his time judgement so he counted from a hundred down to one and felt confident that his dad was not coming out, the room simply could not be large enough, or complex enough, for him to still be checking it out. Cautiously he stood and inched forwards, walking quietly with his eyes on the open doorway, ready to disappear around the gentle curve of the corridor at the first sign of movement from the doorway until he realised he was so close to it there was no way he could disappear back into the patterns and that, in any case, being caught didn't matter, they'd just split the unexplored rooms again.

He walked towards the doorway more purposely and crept

up to the doorway, peeking around it and in. He saw an empty hallway and decided he no longer needed to creep. Just as he stepped into the room he heard voices, not from within the room but from down the corridor.

Isaac was confused. He was sure he'd seen his dad go into the room he was standing just inside of, but it was clearly a man's voice down the corridor.

He walked back out of the room and started edging around the corridor, peeking at what was ahead, the voice was clear enough but weirdly there was other voices too. They sounded like men's voices too, and there was even some clanging and banging.

It was, in truth, a silly thing to do. Unexpected people on the ship were a bad thing no matter what, most likely they were there to work and Andy would get in trouble for letting his family on board. But then again maybe it was Andy and he had come looking for them. Maybe there was a problem and he had bought in some other workers to find them.

Isaac laughed to himself. A hide and seek search party trying to find the hardest people you could try to find, a bunch of kids and an adult just there on this massive ship to hide.

He could see a staircase up ahead and, to his right, a pair of double doors marked with a sign saying *Safe Room*. He could see lights between the cracks of the doors and could now clearly hear a few voices behind it - one much deeper than the others - and they seemed to be arguing, although he couldn't hear what about.

Isaac put his ear against the door and tried to listen but the door was thick and other than the odd word it was muffled.

'...pick...'

'Now lii....'

'When...'

Above all else, Isaac was curious. He was a twelve-year-old boy after all. But he was also naïve. Jack was a fountain of bubbling light and fun. He never thought ill of the world, and so neither did Isaac. Which is why Isaac looked to the side of the door, saw the key pass reader and had an idea.

He felt in his pocket and could feel his pass. There was something behind the door. The door was locked. He wanted to see what was behind the door. He had a piece of plastic that would let him do so.

And so he did.

The doors swung open. Mitchell, Knuckles and Blake stopped talking and looked up at him. The smile dropped off of Isaac's face faster than a coconut off its palm. He might have been raised in a world that was happy and good but he didn't need a second glance to realise these three men were no good.

All three were holding tools of one sort or another, one was very large, one looked very mean, and one looked unbelievably angry.

Luckily, the men were themselves so shocked to see a twelve-year-old boy standing at the doorway of the secure room in an empty ship that they didn't immediately grab him. Instead, they stared dumbstruck which gave Isaac enough time to spin on the spot and run, pounding along the padded carpet to the doorway of the room he'd just left.

He ran into the suite before the men chasing him had managed to put down their equipment and get their bodies through the door into the corridor.

In a blind panic, and trying to be quiet, he leapt into the first room he saw to his left and crawled under the bed, lifting the skirting on it just high enough to peek out at the door to the room.

Isaac thought like a hide and seeker and knew that under the bed was a terrible place to hide, it was the first place anyone looked when they checked a room for someone who was hiding. He scanned the room for anywhere else he could crawl into and saw that the bulkhead up against the corridor had a hatch under it, a hatch that appeared to be just a crack open.

He heard voices from the hallway and made a quick decision.

Chapter 19.

Mitchell looked at Blake, then at Robbie, back to Blake and then back to the door.

There was, he could not deny it, a young boy standing there looking exactly as shocked as he felt. He heard a tiny groan from beside him, Blake slowly realising something was very amiss, and then the boy was gone, disappearing down the corridor to the left.

Mitchell was holding a plan of the safe room in one hand and the exposed end of a wire that was supposed to be connected to a battery in the other. The other end was buried beneath a load of tools in the bag Blake had packed and carried and which was now at his feet as a complicated, knotty hurdle.

He forgot all this and started running to the door, stopping when the wire he held wrapped around Blake's leg and stopped him in his tracks. He turned around, stared at his brother who looked lost for words, and at Robbie, who looked ashen-faced. Mitchell shouted at them. 'What you doin'! Come on!'

Mitchell fled the room and raced down the corridor and round the corner, coming to a stop as he registered the open doors of the rooms he passed. He counted in his head and turned around, beckoning to his brother and Robbie to come closer.

They huddled in the corridor, Mitch whispering at them. 'Listen, doesn't matter how fast that kid was, even Carl Lewis couldn't have made it down further than this and look... some of the doors are open.' He gestured back along the corridor.

'What the heck is going on here? You said this place was empty.' snapped Robbie, his voice low but still audibly angry.

'We saw a boy.' said Blake, in a register that would not have been out of place in a crowded market

Robbie and Mitch both shushed him before Mitch turned to Robbie in a low tone. 'I don't know. It's supposed to be empty. And I would say we should just leave, but given there is one person here who just saw our faces and could describe us to the police, I would not suggest we try and creep out until we find out how many other people are here and make sure we can avoid them.'

'But how? Where did he go?' asked Robbie.

'I don't know, but look at the open doors. He's in one of the rooms. We can find him, there's only so many to look at.'

'Why we whispering?' asked Blake. 'He knows we're here.'

'It's called the element of surprise. He knows we're here...' Mitch gestured so as to encompass the entire ship. 'But he doesn't know we're here.' He pointed down at the ground beneath their feet. 'Look, it doesn't matter, here's the plan. Blake, you stand here and look that way, and if you see him shout, loud, and we'll come. Robbie, you go down there, back where we came from. I'll go room to room and flush him out. Got it? He couldn't be too far from here.'

The two men nodded and started towards their position.

'Wait!' whispered Mitchell loudly. 'Cover your faces!' He pulled up his t-shirt to demonstrate, resting its collar upon his nose so that his face could only be seen from the bridge of his nose and up. The other two nodded and adopted his style.

Mitchell looked left to right. The open doors could be a decoy. After all the kid could have closed a different door quietly. On the other hand, they seemed too obvious to ignore.

He entered the first open door and started searching the rooms.

*

Behind the hatch, Tommo was talking very quietly.

'I can hear him.' he said. 'There was something else too, but someone definitely came into this room and didn't leave again.'

'The carpet is very soft.' whispered back Jack. 'You could have missed it.'

'Not Isaac. He's not at all gentle. I could hear him for certain if he did.'

'Then what's he doing?' chipped in Tabby. 'He's not moving about, do you think he's gone to sleep?'

Sandy shook her head, uselessly, in the dark. 'No, you'd hear him snoring, we all would.'

'Then what?' asked Tommo, more insistently. 'He's not looking for us, do you think we have to go have a look?'

'Let's give him another minute.' said Jack gently. 'He should have a chance to find us if he is there and we just open the door he will see us for certain and it would ruin the game for him.'

They had huddled in the space waiting. They could not see each other well, the sliver of light coming through the seal around the door was barely enough to ward off the pitch darkness that is accompanied by the eyes playing tricks on you.

They all counted, in their heads, and after a minute or so was up Jack reached out and opened the door, not a lot, just a tiny fraction, just enough for the kids to lean around and peer through, into the room, a sliver of carpet, a segment of drape, a slice of bedhead. It was inconclusive.

Tommo reached out, put his hand on Jack's shoulder and whispered in the quietest voice he could muster into Jack's ear. 'Close it. Now.'

He said it with such certainty that Jack obliged. In fact, he more than obliged. Rather than pulling the door back to rest on its catch he fully closed it, firmly, making a very clear click.

The reason Tommo had asked him to close it was because he heard more footsteps, but heavy ones, one's that could not possibly be Isaac's and which were almost certainly those of a full-size man. A man who at that point had entered the room.

He was not a good seeker and had been going through the rooms very broadly, checking under beds and ignoring the more subtle spots all around him. However, there was no doubting that he heard a click to his right in this room.

He surveyed the room and was just about to look under the bed he when he heard a noise from beside the wall. It was quiet but it was clear; a small groan. As he looked at the wall he realised there was a subtle handle set beneath a sign featuring emergency equipment.

He bent down and put his fingers in the handle, pulling the door open as he did. He didn't know what he expected to see, but he certainly did not expect the wave of fart that hit him. He grimaced and looked in, surprised to see not just a boy, but two girls and a man.

'Boys!' he shouted as loud as he can. 'Come here now.'

He was so glad to have found what he was looking for that it did not occur to him that the boy he had just found was completely different to the one he had seen earlier, one who lay very still, and very quiet, under the bed.

Chapter 20.

Sandy, Tommy and Tabby were in a bathroom. They were not locked in, the lock was on the inside, but the very large man was standing in the doorway. They didn't know his name was Blake because both Mitchell and Robbie had been sensible enough to keep their names secret along with their faces. The large guy on the door however did not seem so sharp and had called the others by their names on multiple occasions.

This was why the kids knew that Mitchell and Robbie or, sometimes, Knuckles, were currently interrogating Jack in the living room whilst the larger man kept guard on them.

They whispered amongst themselves with Tommo straining to hear some of the conversation. Even trying as hard as he could all he could register through the walls was an ongoing back and forth and very little detail

'Pssst...' said Tabby, gathering the other two kids towards her. 'Do you think Isaac is still next door?' she whispered conspiratorially, barely breaking the air with her voice.

The bathroom they were in was just up the hallway from the bedroom they'd been in, sandwiched between that room and the master bedroom so they would have been able to hear had Isaac been found. What they couldn't be sure of was whether he had been there in the first place, they only had Tom's strong impression and the arrival of the men had confused things.

When they'd been marched out of the hatch they'd all tried to survey the room as subtly as they could without giving away that they were looking for someone else, and none of them had spotted a sign of him, but then they wouldn't have. It was a frustrating quality the group had, give these circumstances.

The men had surrounded them quickly and frogmarched them all into the bathroom including Jack whilst they'd had a discussion outside the room about what to do next. Eventually, they'd decided they would talk to the adult and had come and got him out.

They'd all listened to the conversation going on outside the door and when it was clear they were going to be split up Jack had quickly turned to Sandy, who was beside him, and whispered in her ear. 'Stay here, but if you leave, Isaac's first spot.'

They knew what that meant of course. They should go to the tube of the largest slide and wait for Jack there if they could get out, but as things stood that looked unlikely. And besides, how could they do that and leave Isaac behind.

'We need to work out if he's there.' said Sandy. 'Maybe we could... crawl through air conditioning ducts? Like they do in movies.'

The looked around. The vents into the bathroom were narrow slits near the walls, with no large opening they could prise open and leave via.

'Wait!' said Tommo. 'I know how!'

He stood up and walked to the sink and flipped the tap on.

The water flowed out smoothly into the white porcelain of the sink. He frowned then went to the bath and tried the tap.

The water came out but there was an audible thrum as it did, the pipes in the walls shaking slightly when the pressure started up.

Tommo closed his eyes and concentrated very hard, his sister and cousin staring at him bemused.

He turned the tap on and off, on for a bit longer and off again, then on and off again. A pause. Then on off, on off, on longer, off. Another pause. Three longer bursts, a pause then a longer, a shorter, a longer.

He turned and pressed his ear against the wall, his eyes still closed.

Tabby started to say something to him but he shushed her quickly with a finger to her lips.

After a few more seconds he smiled.

'He's there.' whispered Tom. 'It's Morse. I said are you okay, I mean R U OK, the letters. He just responded. I think he's scratching on the wall, he said Y, yes it means, the letter Y not the word why.'

'Can we talk to him by scratching? Can he hear us?' asked Sandy.

'Maybe,' said Tommo, 'But he must have crawled out of the bed and over to the wall to do it. It's not safe. I'm going to tell him to go back under the bed. Let's tell him to stay there and stay still. At least we will know where he is.'

Tabby looked concerned. 'What about the slide? Couldn't he hide there? We'd know where he was, he'd be safe, and he wouldn't be here. What if they move us?'

'Tabby's right.' Sandy said. 'We just need to clear the path for him. Create a distraction. Tell him to get ready and go to the slide when he hears my voice. In the corridor. I have a plan.'

'Okay.' said Tommo, thinking about how to say it in as few letters as possible. When he was ready he reached out and started scratching on the wall.

W...e...n... ...u... ...h...e...a...r... ...S... ...g...o... ...t...o... ...s...l...i...d...e...

He waited and then he heard a response, a long scratch, short scratch, long scratch.

'He says 'K. He means Okay, he's ready.'

Sandy walked to the door and knocked on it.

'Who is it?' came a deep voice through the door.

Sandy didn't answer, opening the door instead and looking at the eyes of their guard. In a voice that was louder than her normal speaking voice, a voice she was sure would be heard she said to the man, pointing at Tommo. 'Look at him. That boy there. You see him? He needs to go to the toilet and he can't hold it in anymore. I cannot stay here while he does. No one should have to be in the room while he does.'

The trick worked. The man guarding the door couldn't help gazing at Tommo who cooperated by making a pained expression. Meanwhile, her voice had carried well enough that Isaac had heard it. He peeked out of the bedroom he was in, saw the guards back turned and started through the doorway.

However, Sandy's voice had worked a little too well and drew the attentions of Robbie who leaned his head into the corridor to check on the commotion. As he did so he saw the boy disappear through the door and, not to be caught flat-footed twice, was straight out after him.

Isaac ran fast but was no match for the man chasing him, not with so little head start this time.

A couple of minutes later the bathroom door shut again, this time with all four of the children inside it.

They all hugged Isaac and tried to explain what was going on as best they could. He'd worked most of it out from under the bed, and filled them in on the fact that he'd led the men right to them.

'It was an accident.' said Tabby. 'Very unlucky and you couldn't have known. Don't feel bad.'

'Err....' said Tommo. 'There is a problem though. I really do need to use the toilet this time. The excitement has got me going.'

The knocked on the door again but the man guarding it was not falling for the same trick again and held the door closed by the handle.

'Whatever needs to happen in there,' he said laconically, 'it's going to happen in there.'

'Sorry' said Tommo. 'Could you all turn away?'

Chapter 21.

Jack twitched in his chair, watching Mitchell's hands. The man kept touching him, on the arm, the shoulder, the back, and once on the face. The hands he was watching were very clearly dirty, and Jack could not tell what sort of dirt it was. Presumably, it was just regular, common dirt, whatever that was. But why did it have to come on to him?

Mitchell was pacing in front of him, interrogating him. Like the kids, he knew the man's name was Mitchell thanks to the larger man who was guarding the kids in the bathroom and who did not appear overly bright. Not that Mitchell was much smarter as far as he could tell, even if he did seem to be the leader.

The other man, Robbie, was standing to one side, very still, his sharp eyes serious and studious. He had not really spoken other than yesses and no's and he looked somewhat uncomfortable with his t-shirt pulled up on the bridge of his nose. It was not a good disguise, for a couple of reasons.

Since they were not used to being dressed in this way inadvertent movements kept pulling the t-shirt down and exposing their faces, so Jack knew perfectly well what they looked like. Secondly, the whole thing looked ridiculous and gave the impression that they were, frankly, not very good as criminals, which is what they clearly were.

Jack remembered seeing a film where a sophisticated crew of criminals robbed something or other, but that was called Ocean's Eleven. These guys were the Oceans Three, very fitting given where they were but without any of the competence or smoothness of the people in those films. He smirked.

'And what's so funny?' Mitchell asked, interrupted from his vocal stride by his interrogatee smirking.

'Nothing.' said Jack. 'I was just thinking how it would make sense for one of those Oceans films being set on a cruise ship. You know... elaborate heists with a crack team of canny career criminals... Oceans... cruise ship.'

'Who said we were criminals?' asked Mitchell, waving his hands. 'I don't think that's a fair characterisation at all.'

'Oh, I thought that was a given. I mean, you're obviously not ship's security, you've held us... captive, you're trying to find out from me why I am here, who else knows I am here, if there's any other people here, you know, this whole situation. It really just... I mean come on guys, you've covered your faces, that's very suspicious.'

'I don't think so.' said Mitch indignantly. He turned to Robbie. 'Do you?'

Robbie shook his head and let out a 'Nah.'

'See.' said Mitchell, turning back to Jack and stepping closer to him. 'There's no reason to think we're criminals, or up to no good. None at all.' He reached over and touched Jack's arm, again, with his dirty hands.

That touch was a trigger, enough to set something off in Jack. Defiance with a twist of payback. 'I'll tell you what I would have done in your situation.' He began, leaning back so that Mitchell's hand disengaged with his arm. 'For starters, I would not have chased us at all, or hidden our faces. I'd have put on an official tone. I mean, you're dressed in jeans, dungarees, work clothes. I would have claimed you were mechanics or crew working on the ship, maybe in for repairs. Then I would have escorted us all to a holding area, somewhere open and comfortable, but a little out of the way. A dining room, somewhere like that. I would have said that it wasn't safe to be on the ship right now, but that once you'd finished your emergency repair work you'd escort us off and then left and done.. whatever it was you were going to do.

'As it is I think you panicked. You acted like someone caught doing something they shouldn't have, which really we had no reason to think. Sure, maybe that story would have unravelled and we'd have had our suspicions but compared to just... chasing us, dragging us out, separating us, putting the kids in the bathroom, I mean come on guys, come on. How do you think that looks?'

Mitchell gave Jack a very peculiar look. Perhaps it would have made more sense accompanied by the rest of its facial expression but with nothing but eyes to go on, it was simply peculiar. He stood up, beckoned to Robbie and took him over to the other side of the lounge room. They debated between themselves in low voices for a few back-and-forth's until they seemed to come to a decision.

Mitchell strode over and took Jack by the arm. 'Come on.' He ordered, bringing him to his feet and walking him to the door of the main bedroom that led off from the lounge. He sat him on the bed and told him to stay there and left, coming back a few moments later followed by a line of silent children who marched into the room and ran to Jack, all hugging him at once.

'Stay here.' said Mitchell. 'And no funny business.'

He closed the door and Jack checked they were all okay. They relayed what had happened, how they'd communicated with Isaac and how he'd almost escaped to the slide.

'Don't worry.' said Jack. 'We'll be fine, even if this has ruined our game a bit. We just need to figure out what these guys are planning on doing. I don't think they're that sharp or prepared for this, they obviously thought the ship would be deserted.'

'What about Andy?' asked Tabby. 'Why did he let them in?'

'Good question. I imagine they gave him no choice, but we can worry about that later. Right now I think we could use your ears, Mr Isaac. At the door, if you could?'

Isaac saluted and walked quietly to the door, putting his ear up against it and blocking the other ear with a finger.

Meanwhile, Tommy pulled on Jack's elbow until he got his attention.

'What is it?' whispered Jack.

'I have a plan.' said Tommo.

Chapter 22.

'I don't like this.' said Robbie. 'Don't like this at all. They've seen us all.'

'Don't worry about that.' snapped Mitchell. 'Look, Blake, go to the safe room, take the pass. In the black bag is some masks. Face masks, the white ones, for dust. Bring them back will you.'

'Sure thing.' said Blake, taking the pass and trotting out the suite.

As soon as he was gone Mitchell got very serious and failed to keep his voice as low as he might have. 'Straight up, don't worry about it. Me, you, we match the description of thousands of people. We checked him, we checked the kids, one phone, no service, we have it now anyway so no problem, I don't know about his hide and seek business, but really what else are they but trespassers. They should not be here and the fact is we know who he is, where he lives and what his blooming kids look like, so I don't think he's no trouble if we play this right.'

'But what if there's more?' asked Robbie. 'There could be people everywhere, behind every curtain and who knows. We don't know it's safe.'

'This is our big payday Knuckles. We can make this work. You need to get back to that safe room and get to work. I'll get Blake to look after them here and I'll do a recce, make sure we're alone. The biggest problem we've had so far is delays. The guy in the booth, whatever his name is, he's got a shift and at some point someone will realise he's not where he's meant to be. You know what you need to do so get to it.'

'Sure thing.' said Robbie. 'But I don't want to be standing with the torch in my hand, turn round and find the entire police force standing behind me, nor a load more kids. You work out if anyone else is here, plus, you work out an alternate escape plan, and you come and tell me. I'll work like the clappers until then. Deal.'

Mitchell extended his hand and shook Robbie's. 'No problems, will do.'

Robbie left the suite, bumping into Blake on the way out and taking a face mask off him. Blake came to his brother and handed another over, the last already on his face.

'Better.' said Mitchell. 'We have a plan now. Listen, I need you to stay right here, where I am, outside this door, and under no circumstances can you let these people leave this room understand?'

'Sure bro.' said Blake. 'But what if the kids need the toilet.'

'Fine, they can leave for the toilet. But nothing else.'

'What if they're hungry?' continued Blake.

'Tough.' said Mitchell.

'What if they get bored?'

'I don't care! They can be bored and hungry, they just got to stay in this room. We have to contain this. We keep them there, we get our job done, we get out. We can still make this work, we just have to be careful and you just have to stay here.'

'Yes.' said Blake, knowing from Mitchell's tone that this was not a moment for more questions.

'Good. Now you stand right here and I will be back in five minutes got it?'

'Got it.'

Mitchell slapped his brother on the back and stalked out the room, his head swimming.

It seemed clear enough what they needed to do, as long as there were no more surprises. They finish doctoring the safe room so they can get in later and make sure it looks like a botched attempt to rig the door. Simple, the investigators will come in and maybe they replace the door, but the safe boxes themselves they won't touch, it'll be a perfect double bluff, that what will make the plan work.

They still needed to be very careful to not leave any fingerprints or evidence. No problems, that was standard operating procedure.

Put a bit of pressure on this guy, make it clear there'll be a problem if he says anything and they should be fine. No different to the guy at the door. In fact, it's even better to have these guys here. Even if they do squeal to the coppers then so what? Same outcome. The cops will see the obvious door tampering and think they've found the whole problem, they won't expect the bait and switch.

Mitchell stalked back up the stairs following the blue, then the red line until he was out on the deck near the gantry entrance. He surveyed the scene. Everything looked calm.

Mitchell pulled out his walkie-talkie and buzzed Kenny in the booth.

'Kenny, you there? Over.'

'Yes boss. ' came the tinny reply.

'We have a problem here. We got a family, a bloke and four kids, onboard, running about. They claim they're just playing a game of hide and seek. We have them locked up now. Over.'

'You say hide and seek?'

'Don't worry about that. Listen, is that guy we knocked out awake yet? Over.'

'That's a negative.'

'Fine. Can you go for a walk, please. Go find where the cars are parked. I need to know how many cars there are. There's five of them, they must have got here somehow. Over.'

'Sure thing' said Kenny.

There was a delay of a minute or so before the walkie jumped back into life. 'Mitch you there?'

'Yes, I am. What you seeing? Over.'

'Two cars here. One has plenty of evidence of kids, the other one is pretty clean.'

'Great.' said Mitchell. 'I think we have the problem contained. Sit tight, let me know if there're any issues. Over.'

'Sure thing.'

Mitchell clenched his fist and punched the air. There was no one else aboard. They had the situation under control. He was a positive guy. He was seeing nothing but rainbows in his future. Rainbows and money. Rainbows, money, and a cruise.

*

Kenny Deans finished walking around the cars and was making his way back to the booth when he felt a shiver run down his spine. It was a feeling, indistinct but clear enough, the feeling he'd had a few times in his life of the walls closing in, of the game being up, of him being about to meet a judge.

Kenny walked calmly back to the booth and put the walkie-talkie down on the side and then went to the man on the floor, checking his pockets and finally pulling out his keys. He checked the ropes were secure, took the man's phone and dropped it in his pocket and went back to the cars, getting into the clean one and driving out of the dry dock.

He watched the van, the dirty kid car, the ship and the booth disappear in his rearview mirror.

If things didn't go south and anyone asked, he'd say he saw something, he could make it up, he was a good liar. Until then the only thought he had was getting as far away from the scene as possible.

Half a kilometre down the road he threw the booth man's phone out the window and on he drove, his gloved hands clinging to the steering wheel, his eyes on freedom.

Chapter 23.

Mitchell followed the lines back down into the ship with a skip in his step. The plan remained on. They were alone again, not as alone as they would have liked but alone enough.

Most important he felt back in control. He had one guy on the gate, making sure nothing was coming at them from outside. He had a man on these interlopers, making sure nothing was coming at them from the inside. He had Robbie doing his magic in the safe room. All he had to do was work out how to get out of there if they did find themselves in a pinch, unlikely, and he was back in control.

Mitchell stopped in on Robbie and saw him hard at work with a gas torch. He gestured at him, showed all five fingers on one hand to indicate five minutes, and one finger on the other to indicated waiting, then mouthed 'give me five' as Robbie looked up.

He took the schematics of the ship and went back to the suite where he found Blake still standing at the door to the master bedroom.

He put the plans down on the table in the lounge room and spread them out, trying to make sense of them. From what he could see there was only one way on and off the ship, but he was hoping he could find an alternative.

The ship was rigged with a load of lifeboats which were connected to winches that lowered them down to the water. That might work.

He went out on to the balcony and looked towards the back of the boat where the giant dock doors kept the sea at bay. What he needed was a pair of binoculars because they were so far away but all he had was the phone on his camera and its zoom function.

He zoomed in as well as he could and watched the shaky, grainy footage. He was sure. There was a staircase there, leading up the doors, and on to a walkway across the top of them. The dock itself was massive, it gave them a chance.

Worst case scenario some police or security burst in and they flee to the other side of the deck and into a lifeboat, lower themselves down. The hull of the ship would let them hide underneath it and then dash to the dock doors. They'd have enough time to get to the stairs and up and away if they had to. It was not foolproof, but there was an escape which meant Mitchell was feeling particularly in control of things.

He slapped the plans on the table happily and went to tell Robbie the plan, before coming back to discuss it with Blake.

'Given the circumstances, we've been looking at our Plan B and I think we're good.' He said, happily. 'Any problems we head to the other side of the ship and... well... you just follow me, I've got us covered okay. We're still good.'

'Yes brother.' said Blake. 'But what about the room. The safe room?'

'Knuckles is on it, he knows what to do. He'll get that door looking badly messed up, that won't take long, and then he can do the real job with the boxes. You just need to go and help him at the end get everything out of there okay? We're fine.'

'Yes brother.' said Blake again. There were parts of the plan he understood and parts he didn't, but he knew that Mitch didn't like explaining again and again.

'Now listen, any trouble in there?'

'Not a peep, been quiet as mice, I haven't heard a thing.'

Mitchell smiled then stopped still. 'Literally nothing? Have you checked on them?'

'No. you told me to stay here and not let them out.'

'For crying out loud...' said Mitchell, barging past his brother and into the bedroom.

The entire room was deserted, not a soul to be seen. Meanwhile, the doors to the balcony were open. Mitchell rushed to them and looked both ways. To his left, on the divider that separated this balcony with the next, was the clear imprint of a shoe. They'd got loose in the ship and headed he didn't know where.

They would not have had enough time to get all the way back to their car yet and he couldn't see them, which meant they were still on the ship or trying to get out.

'Blake! They've escaped you blooming idiot. Come on, follow me!'

Mitchell ran from the room, his brother trailing after him. They flew down the corridor to the stairs, up to the red line and then out to the deck and the gantry. Mitchell scanned the horizon in every direction.

'They couldn't have got out.' he said. 'You stay here, do not let anyone pass and talk to Kenny. Let him know we have some rats on the loose. I'll try and flush them out.' Mitchell tossed the walkie-talkie at his brother and ran back down into the ship.

Blake watched him leave, frowned, then lifted the walkie talkie to his mouth. 'Kenny, listen, we lost that man and kids, you just keep an eye out for them and let me know if you see them.' He paused for a second and lifted the device back to his lips. 'Over' he finished, happy with his contribution, and utterly unconcerned that he had not received any reply. He'd done the talkie, the listenie didn't seem important.

Blake pulled off his mask, put it in his pocket, sighed deeply and stood sentry.

Chapter 24.

The bedroom room was quiet. Too quiet. It was the sort of quiet that told you someone or something was there being quiet. You needed a certain type of ear, a certain knack, a sixth-and-a-half sense to discern it but it was there, hanging in the room like the lingering after-scent of perfume after a grandma has left.

Suddenly the silence was broken.

'They're gone.' said a ruffle of curtain.

Isaac emerged from the curtain, checking carefully and listening again. He couldn't hear anyone, anywhere, other than the people in the room with him.

Slowly the others came out of hiding.

Jack had been under the bed but not lying on the floor like a noob. He'd wedged himself into the bed's frame, hooking his feet and hands under slats so that he was not making any contact with the ground, a classic hide.

The dresser drawer opened by its own devices and a fair hand emerged, pulling on the drawer above until the drawer was out enough for Tabby to pop her head out and carefully climb out. She was helped since unlike most chests of drawers this one was both capacious and screwed down to the floor.

The door of the wardrobe beside the door to the room swung open and from within it came Tommo, unfolding himself from a deep low shelf where he'd been hidden at the back, out of sight from adult eye level.

Finally, from the top of the wardrobe came Sandy, carefully lowering herself down and dusting herself off. The suite may well have been one of the more luxurious on the ship, but the cleaning, as elsewhere, did not extend to the parts where no one ever looked.

They regrouped in the middle of the room and Jack gave them all silent high fives, smiling at each, and reserving a special hug for his nephew, Tommo, for coming up with their brilliant plan.

Isaac whispered to them all. 'I think I know what they are doing here. I think I heard them.'

'That doesn't matter now.' said Jack, 'we just need to get off the ship without being caught.'

'I don't think that will work.' said Tabby. 'I know they don't seem that smart, but surely they would have realised that there's only one way on and off this ship. They'd have to be one of them standing there.'

'I'm worried about your friend.' said Sandy. 'he wouldn't have let them in would he, he might be in trouble. We should try and help him.'

'I think Andy will be okay.' said Jack thoughtfully. 'He can certainly look after himself. But I agree with you, I'm worried about him too, and about all of you. I'm not sure how we get out of this. We can hide until they leave I guess, I think they'll be keener on getting whatever they are doing done and escaping than on catching us again. They probably just want to make sure they get out of here before we do so we can't call the police.'

'But how long will that be?' Tommo asked. 'We could be here all night. I don't want to sleep here.' He sounded sad but then he looked around the luxurious room. 'Well, I wouldn't mind sleeping here, but I don't think we should.'

'You're right.' Jack said. 'Of course. And there is a bigger problem. They know everything about me. They've taken my driver's license, they have my phone, they know where I live, where we all live and they told me, in no uncertain terms, that they would be you know... coming for me, for us, if we said a word.'

Sandy gasped. 'But we can't let them get away with it, can we? We have to get out of here and tell the police. It's not fair otherwise. If the police have them we will be safe at least.'

'I don't know what to say.' Jack shrugged. 'Your safety comes first. You're my responsibility all of you, your mum and dad trusted me to look after you too.' He indicated his niece and nephew. 'I think our priority has to be getting out of here. And before that, I really think we need to get out of this room.'

'Hold on.' said Tabby. 'I have an idea, let's find a room down the corridor and I'll explain it.'

They moved cautiously through the room and down the hallway to the corridor, looking both ways before Jack beckoned them out and to the left. They marched quietly down the corridor, past the first suite they had entered and stopped eventually at a double-doors with windows in it that led to an internal staircase.

Quietly as he could, Jack pushed it open, and Isaac put his head through, listening intently before signalling that it was safe, and leading them through.

When they reached the top floor and could see daylight outside Tabby explained her plan. It was simple enough. 'The problem we face is an easy one.' she said. 'It's just a game of back to base when you think about it.'

Chapter 25.

Mitchell tore around the top deck looking everywhere he could see before deciding that the man and kids were not outside.

He wasn't surprised to not find them but he was disappointed at himself. He was panicking and running around like a headless chicken instead of stopping and thinking. He was meant to be the mastermind in the group, that was his whole schtick. That's why he could turn up with no knowledge, no useful skills, not even muscles, and still be a part of the team. He was the thoughts behind it.

Which meant that he could certainly outsmart a bunch of kids and one guy who was stupid enough to take a load of kids on to a vacated ship. He just had to outthink them.

Mitchell was on the side of the ship facing away from the gantry that led them on board. He sat on a bench fitted to a wall and stared out at the distance. There was nothing ahead of him but the blue sky. The sun was shining but he was in the shade. It was warm enough, cool enough, he could take a moment. He took off his mask and put it in his jacket pocket. He breathed the sea air and felt a moment of calmness wash into him.

Blake had the only exit guarded, Knuckles had the safe room under control, all that mattered was that they got away before the kids. They could burst the tires on their car to stop them following, basically just strand them.

It wouldn't hurt them, they'd be fine, and so would he be. He felt Jack's phone in his pocket and pulled it out. It still showed dead air, just the emergency signal showing. The guy seemed clever enough to take the hint, he had not made an explicit threat but he'd made it clear that he knew where he lived.

Surely that was enough. Why would he care about the ship? All he had to do was keep his mouth shut, say he saw and heard nothing, and he could walk away along with his kids.

I wonder, thought Mitchell to himself, *If I would go over and threaten him? Would I follow through?*

He thought for a moment and decided that he wouldn't. It was too risky for one thing, and also he didn't really like violence or getting his hands dirty.

But would he send Blake over? Or pay a guy to go shove a threatening note through the door? For sure he would.

The next question then was whether the guy, Jack, thought he would do it. He'd locked them all up, but he hadn't hurt anyone. He'd made it clear that win-win was that they both walked out when the time was right and didn't look back. He'd suggested violence. He threatened it, but he hadn't followed through.

Could he have punched him or broken a finger? Maybe. But that was classless to Mitchell's mind. Especially with his kids around. Classless but also, he realised, weakness, something he should not have shown.

He stood up and stretched out his back. What was done was done, he could only look forwards now, make sure that they did everything they could and got out of there.

If they'd known the kids were there would they have still come? No.

Now they were here should they abandon? No!

What did that leave really? The kids were running around the ship. So what? They couldn't go anywhere. In fact, the other thing he really had to worry about was making sure Robbie got everything he needed to get done, done.

He started walking back around the deck until he found the red line on the floor leading through the door. He could see Blake standing immobile guard in the distance, an Easter Island statue uprooted and put on the deck. Mitchell waved at him but Blake was lost in his own thoughts, whatever they were.

Mitchell went inside and made his way back down to the safe room, arriving to the sound of a blow torch, the heavy smell of smoke and the heat coming off the door.

Robbie turned off the torch and hung the handle on the hook that came off the canister, pulling off his glasses.

'How you going Knuckles?' asked Mitchell.

'Good mate, all done here. I'll let it cool off and double-check but think it's fine, just need to clean it up.'

'Great. How long for the safe boxes then?'

'Maybe twenty minutes, then have a tidy, finish up here then need to pack it all away. You got those kids under control?'

'Sure thing.' said Mitchell. 'They won't be bothering you again, don't worry about it, you just do what you have to. I'll send Blake down in half an hour to help you okay? We're just keeping watch up on deck, just in case, but we got our plan B sorted out, don't worry about that. From now on we're back on the plan, nothing will get in our way.'

Robbie gave the okay sign and moved into the room containing the safe deposit boxes, addressing a panel neatly recessed into the wall.

Mitchell turned and headed back to the stairs, back to Blake to update him and eventually take over from him. As he climbed the stairs for what felt like the hundredth time that day he felt tired, exhausted almost. This was meant to be an easy job. But it didn't matter. He was the mastermind, he could adjust.

Chapter 26.

Tommo was fast for his age. He was only nine but neither of his parents could keep up with him. His dad could still beat him over very short distances, but when they raced he only ever won by a head at most. If Tommo had any sort of head start he was never caught.

On top of that, he had endurance. He couldn't run a marathon, or even a half-marathon, but give him a five-kilometre course and he could keep going without stopping. He wasn't particularly athletic, and this wasn't something that he felt, of himself, was impressive, he was just a lively nine-year-old boy; these were facts about most lively nine-year-old boys.

This is why he'd been chosen as the bait. He'd volunteered really. Once he heard Tabby's plan he knew he was the right person for it.

He poked his head out of the doors and looked down the deck at the large man by the entranceway.

They'd travelled through the inside of the ship back to where they'd first entered it and he knew the layout of where he was going, what he needed to do.

The man at the gantry was standing very still looking straight ahead, focusing on the wall ahead of him. He didn't seem to have noticed the boy yet so Tom came out completely on to the deck, keeping one foot through the door, holding it open.

The man didn't seem to notice him still.

They'd worked out the one flaw in the plan, that the man might not have an access pass on him. He had to come through with Tommo, be right behind him.

Tommo coughed quietly, centred himself, and then let out a much louder shout. 'Hey!' he shouted to the man.

The large head slowly turned and for a second there was nothing in those eyes at all, just a blank expression that slowly gave way to recognition. 'Hey.' came a booming reply. 'What you doing?'

'I need help.' shouted Tommo. 'My uncle, he's hurt, he fell.'

'Come here.' Blake called.

'I can't. I have to keep the door open because I don't have a pass. Do you?'

'No.' said Blake, starting, without realising it, to move towards the boy. 'What's happened?'

'I need your help. My uncle...'

'No. I need you to come to me. I need to keep you somewhere... safe and quiet.' Despite his words, Blake was still walking towards Tommo.

This was more difficult than Tommo had thought. He'd assumed he'd be seen and then chased, he had not counted on an ongoing discussion. Luckily he was a nine-year-old boy and had other tricks in up his sleeve. 'You can't catch me anyway. You're too slow. Too slow and too fat.'

'Hey. I'm not fat.' said Blake, coming alive and quickening his step. 'You come here.'

'No, you come here, if you can, if you're not too stupid.'

'You respect adults hear me.' said Blake, speeding up again, almost joining the boy.

'Not you.' said Tommo, throwing the door open. 'Don't need to, you can't catch me anyway.'

Tommo spun on the spot and was gone, catching Blake by surprise, though not for long. He was big and slow in some ways, but Blake was surprisingly fast on his feet. Blake burst through the doorway just behind Tom but he just couldn't catch him. Steadily the boy was getting away.

Blake wasn't thinking, he was running, chasing, determined to catch the boy as the went through another door and came out into the tall expanse of the deserted lobby.

Tommo was thinking, thinking about where he needed to go next. He knew he'd made headway on the large man but he was calculating in his head and realised it wasn't enough. Instead of heading straight for the intended doorway he made a beeline for the large circular reception desk and banked around it in a large circle. The man followed him.

The gambit worked, straight lines seemed to suit the man's stride better, introducing the large curve around the reception desk slowed him down as his mass pushed him further out than the tight circle Tommo could turn in.

He came back round to the front of the desk and shot off towards the casino, disappearing through its open doors into the dark interior.

Blake came in a few seconds later and rattled to a stop. The whole place was deserted, he'd been had. Keeping his eyes on the doors he started edging into the large room, his eyes adjusting slowly to the minimal lighting provided through the few windows.

Tommo was ready. He was in the igloo, his eyes on the door, calculating again. He'd got lucky, the man had headed in the opposite direction to him, moving to the other side of the room slowly. When he saw his gap he crept out of the igloo and headed for the door again, creeping across the room until he was behind the last table before the doors.

The man turned to look away and Tommo leapt across the floor and through the doors.

Blake turned and started running again, running as fast as could but the gap was too large. Tommo disappeared through the doors. A split second later three small people emerged from the shrubs beside the doors and quickly pulled them to, slamming them closed.

Jack arrived a second later with an Eskimo's spear and jammed it through the handles, effectively locking the door from the outside.

Blake got there a few moments later and started yanking on the doors, trying to get them open but the makeshift locking mechanism held. Until he found another way out he was trapped.

Chapter 27.

Maggie was singing to herself as she drove. She did love to sing when she was alone in the car. She sang out of tune, often with the wrong words, and far too loud, but it upset no one and entertained her.

She would happily skip between music from any of the decades she'd been alive but her heyday was definitely the nineteen-nineties, with the rise of indie bands, girl power, R&B going mainstream and of course the power rock. She'd found her radio station that afternoon and had been belting out the greatest hits of Aerosmith, Queen, Bon Jovi, Cold Chisel and everything else that had come on. The songs, the mood in the car (her own) and the country air had all combined to make her feel better, whatever her ailment had been subsiding to nothing more than a slight giddiness, a dripping nose and the occasional sneezes.

The sun was shining down on her, a beautiful day that turned in to mid-afternoon with a balmy haze on the horizon all around, a sight she could appreciate as she broached the top of a hill and looked down at the shipyard below, a vast acreage dominated by the hulking presence of the cruise ship in the middle of the dry dock.

She could see the road as it wound down the hill through the sheep paddocks, all the way to the entrance gate and booth, and then the various mechanical bits and pieces The whole thing looked deserted, like a scene from a film where people awake from comas to find the entire world deserted with no clue why.

As she came down the hill the scene narrowed until she reached the same level as the dockyards, the ship up ahead looming above her now through the fencing. It was bigger than she had thought it would be. She had seen many cruise ships, but somehow, in this isolated environ, it seemed bigger, more dramatic.

She rolled up to the booth. The gate was up and open and it was deserted as far as she could tell, the door closed. She beeped once for good measure but there was no sign of anyone so she drove on through the gate, assuming that the man at the gate, who she recalled Jack knew, was inside with them all. Maybe he was even joining in, Jack had a way of convincing people of things.

Behind the booth, she found a small parking lot and saw Jack's car there along with a van and pulled up next to it. She went through her handbag quickly, collected her phone, a packet of nasal decongestant sweets she'd bought when she'd stopped for petrol and a packet of tissues, then stuffed them in her handbag headed out the car and started walking down to the ship, heading for the large gantry near its middle.

She did not notice that the van did not have any number plates or that the windows were remarkably tinted, after all, why would she? She'd expected to find a couple of cars and she had.

As Maggie reached the staircase leading up to the gantry she popped a sweet in her mouth, blew her nose and started her ascent. It was more stairs than she'd been expecting. The size of the ship had tricked her, it was so unusually large that she had kept expecting it would stop getting larger as she got closer to it. Now it was a vast tower of metal above her, a daunting climb.

She pulled out her phone and called Jack as she walked, but the phone went straight to his voice mail. As she stared at it and wondered if she should try again she noticed, belatedly, the battery was critically low. In response, the phone promptly turned itself off before her eyes. Didn't matter, she thought, he'd see her car if they somehow missed each other, and even if they did leave, it wasn't the end of the world.

By the time she reached the top of the stairs and crossed the gantry she'd realised that the issue of finding them was more significant than she'd considered. The five of them were hiding somewhere on the ship, and as she well knew they were very good at hiding. How on earth was she going to find them?

The problem then presented itself more significantly to her. She'd walked to the first set of doors and tried to enter it and then discovered it was locked. She walked along the deck and tried the next set, also locked. Just to be sure she went further along, trying doors towards the front of the ship that had a red line leading through them from the deck. Just as locked.

It had not occurred to Maggie that she might be stymied so simply, but she was good at thinking on her feet. She decided to walk around the outside of the ship. Hopefully she would find an open door or if not she would hear something. Better yet, she thought, she could just knock on every door she passed.

Either one of the kids or Jack would open it for her or, eventually, she would end up back where she started and could just wait there. She started walking around. Walking, knocking, calling out, waiting ten seconds, walking some more.

Very quickly she realised it was a very big ship. It had pools, three water slides and a surfing machine and who knew what else! Still, her plan was a good one, and she couldn't do anything else, so she walked and knocked and called out and waited.

Chapter 28.

Jack stood back and watched the door to the casino.

He could see the face of the large man through one of the windows. The door rattled but didn't open, the Eskimos spear was mainly decorative but it was also made of solid metal.

After a few seconds of fruitless shaking, the rattling stopped and the face at the window disappeared.

'Right.' said Jack. 'I don't know how long we've got but I think we need to get out of here as quick as possible. Follow me, and do not stop because...'

Jack was interrupted by a huge smashing sound coming from the door. He jumped, as did the kids, startled, and turned to see what the commotion was. The large man had evidently managed to find a fire extinguisher and was now using it to try and smash through the glass windows of the doors.

They looked like security glass but the sound of the crashing didn't give the security much hope against the brute strength from within. Jack stopped explaining and just started running, making sure all four kids were right on his tail. They went back down the service corridor towards the door to the deck and he buzzed them through.

The door opened and he stepped out. There in front of him on the deck was Mitchell who'd come to find his brother and had found an unprotected gantry instead. Mitchell had started walking around the ship, calling out Blake's name when the man they'd caught, Jack, suddenly came ducking out a door.

They locked eyes for a second, separated by ten meters of the deck. Jack stopped dead and threw out his arms to grab the four kids pouring out the door around him. He managed to stop them and get them moving backwards again and he slammed the door shut yelling at them to follow him.

Jack ran back into the lobby and around the reception desk once more, heading for the main concourse to the far side, desperately trying to think on his feet and remember the exits that they could use.

Mitchell reached the lobby area as they disappeared through the opening at the other end and slowed to a walk. He was trying to remember the plans. Chasing these kids was crazy. They were faster than him, and fitter, and were sneaky little hiders.

Being outrun by them was bag enough but being outthought was much worse, the one thing he had that he knew they didn't was his wits and his lifetime of running from things. If he chased them they could double back around and get off the ship. Maybe Robbie was done with his work, maybe not. Either way, he only had to buy some time. Sure they could run around, but as long as they didn't leave, as long as they didn't get help, he didn't need to worry.

Too late, he realised, he'd not covered his face, the mask still in his jacket pocket. Identification was inevitable now, he could only hope his threats had been enough, but the smart move was to head back to the entrance and wait until Blake came back, or until Robbie came looking for him.

He turned and headed back the way he'd come, to the deck, walking down the service corridor. As he got near the door he started to hear footsteps behind him, lots of them. He turned around and waited. First one, the red-headed girl, and then all four kids, came into view and stopped staring at him in shock. The man, Jack, came running up behind and looked similarly surprised, and then crestfallen.

They stood motionless in front of him, not doing anything, when another sound became clear, the heavy thudding footsteps of his brother who lumbered into the corridor and stopped, panting and sweating. Blake looked over at him, noticed he seemed to be holding one of his hands like it was hurt, and gave him a nod. Blake nodded back.

'That,' said Mitchell. 'is game, set and match I believe. Maybe three, four of you can get out of here but you're not all getting out so how about we come to an understanding. I can see you're having a real delightful field trip, but I'm afraid the time for fun and games is over. We don't want to hurt anyone, not at all, we're just a maintenance crew here doing a bit of work, and we just need you out of the way while we finish up and then you're free to carry on whatever it is you're doing.'

Mitchell stared into Jack's eye and gave his hardest, most steel-like stare. 'It's for your own safety you understand. We can't have anything happening to you because you're in our way.' Mitchell pronounced every word as clearly as he good without breaking eye contact.

Reluctantly Jack, who had been defiant, dropped his head a little and nodded, showing he understood the implied threat. 'You're right.' he said. 'Kids, come on. Let's do what these croo... these maintenance men are asking. Let's go somewhere out of their way and safe until they're finished.'

'But...' started Sandy before Jack silenced her with a hand on the shoulder and a gentle squeeze.

'It's okay kids. We have to do this. Quiet now.' soothed Jack.

Mitchell smiled and changed his tone, appearing far too friendly. 'You'll understand of course that we might need to find somewhere a little more secure for you guys since you seem to be quite good at getting under our feet. I think I know the place, follow me please.'

Mitchell turned and led them out the door on to the

walkway and into the parts of the ship he had some memory of. As he led, followed by the kids and Jack, and with Blake bringing up the rear, they went through the doors with the red lines and down one level, following a sign he'd seen earlier when they'd first come on board.

He stopped outside a room and buzzed it with his pass, opening the door. He poked his head in and seemed satisfied with what he saw. The sign above the door said Morgue.

'I think you'll find this comfortable enough. Lots of hidey-holes, if you can stomach them, one door in and out, I think as well...' he held up his pass and waved it at them... 'you have some of these. If you could hand them over as you go in.'

With death stares and holding back tears in some cases, the kids trooped in, handing over their key passes to Mitchell as they did so. Jack came last and stopped to talk quietly to Mitchell as he handed his pass over.

'You understand,' whispered Jack, 'that if anything happens to any of these kids I will never, ever stop until I find you.'

Mitchell sneered, an ugly sneer of victory. 'That's what the last guy said.' he whispered back. Mitchell put a hand on

Jack's shoulder and pushed him through the door, slamming it after him.

The door clicked closed with the buzzer sound. Mitchell stared at the door for a second then took off down the corridor, coming back with a fire extinguisher with a long rubber hose and used it to tie a complicated messy lock around the handles.

'That should hold them.' said Mitchell. 'You okay brother?'

Blake nodded. 'Maybe a broken finger, nothing to worry about.'

'Great. I need you to get down to Robbie and start helping him get everything outside and tidy up, just do what he tells you okay. Give me the walkie-talkie, I'll keep an eye on these guys and check in on Kenny.

Wordlessly Blake handed over the walkie-talkie and then trotted off down the corridor to the staircase and down the stairs. Mitchell watched him go then checked the door one last time before wandering down the corridor in the opposite direction. 'Kenny, you there mate? Over.'

There was no response.

'Kenny? Over.'

Still no response.

Mitchell came to a staircase and climbed it, in case the ship was blocking them out. 'Kenny? You there? Over.'

Mitchell had reached the top of the staircase now and was about to try again when he heard a weird noise from down the corridor. As far as he could tell he was back on the main deck where they'd started, although over on the other side of the ship. That meant there should not be anyone here. Unless... there were more kids.

He went towards the sound but it moved further away, got quieter, but still clear. A knocking and then a voice? A lady's voice.

Mitchell raced down a corridor to try and get ahead of the sound and made it to a door that had windows out to the deck. He hid in the shadows and looked out the window. He heard the noise again but still distant. He waited some more. A lady appeared in the window and knocked patiently three times loudly.

She was a pleasant enough looking lady, kind eyes, bright

red nose. 'Hello?' she called and waited.

On an impulse, Mitch stepped forwards to the window. 'Hello.' he said.

The lady locked eyes with him, let out a scream and then started running.

'This again!' Mitch exclaimed, unlocking the door and setting off in pursuit. He was getting tired of all this running, he certainly wasn't well dressed for it.

Chapter 29.

In the booth, on the floor, lay Andy. He didn't know he was on the floor but he knew he was somewhere. That in itself might not appear impressive, but having been very much unconscious for some hours it was a vast improvement.

In the vague darkness of his mind, the world was punctuated by a noise. It was a funny noise, a distinct noise, and one that he recognised but could not place. He strained his brain meats to try and put his mental finger on quite what it was but the effort was too much and he lapsed back under to unconsciousness.

Suddenly light filled the world, not a lot but a little. His eyes had opened of their own accord, surprising him. At first, he wasn't sure what light was, but he seemed to remember quickly and he wondered why the wall he was leaning against was so heavy.

A car horn. He suddenly thought. *I heard a car horn.*

This fact in itself seemed incredibly meaningful but he slowly came to realise that it was not so meaningful really. The problem was it was the only thought he had. It towered above the rest of his mental processes, giving it the impression of immense, deep importance, but really, it was just a horn, and he knew that something being 'just a' was a thing too.

This was also very profound.

As he lay there, his eyes a little open, something in his brain did something clever. It took the entire world and shifted it into its proper place. The heavy wall to his right became a floor and he came to understand that he was lying down.

He tried to move but couldn't. He didn't know why and thought he might be injured but his faculties were quickly coming back to him now and he managed to work out in short order that the only part of him that hurt was his head, that he could not move because he was tied up with something and that something bad had happened to him to lead to this.

He lay there thinking about the implications of all this when a new noise came into the booth, which he quickly recognised was his booth. He was at work.

'Kenny, you there mate?' came a voice from somewhere in the room.

Andy didn't know a Kenny, but he knew that the sound was that of a walkie talkie, which meant there was a walkie talkie in the room. Things began to materialise in his mind. A van. Some kids. A pain in his head.

'Kenny?' Over.' It was the voice again. They were looking for Kenny. Andy didn't know a Kenny. Then again, he wasn't sure that he was sure that he didn't know a Kenny. He did now know he was Andy.

With an almighty effort, Andy rolled on to his stomach, bent his legs and managed to stand up, quickly flopping uncomfortably into his chair as a wave of light-headedness hit him. His arms were tied behind his back, which meant he was leaning on his forearms. The ties, he could now see, were ropes, cutting into his wrists.

From this position, he could see his normal outlook. Console, windows, gate, ship. That was all familiar, but there was something that wasn't. The thing making the noise.

'Kenny. You there? Over.' it said.

The pieces started falling in to place. Jack and his kids had come and then this van. Jack should not have been there but that was not bad, well, it was, but a different sort of bad. Not the tie you up and bash you on the head sort of bad.

With his clarity returning he got to his feet, hopping on his bound legs. He looked out at the ship but there was nothing unusual there. He checked the car park. His car was gone but Jack's was still there, and the van and, weirdly, a whole new car.

Whoever had been minding him had clearly gone for a walk so this was his chance.

One of the benefits of spending hours every day in a tiny little room is that you come to know it very well. For example, you know that there is a box cutter in the top drawer to your on the left. Andy hopped over and turned his back to it and then squatted, opening the draw with difficult and then fishing around in it blindly until he could feel the thick plastic handle of the cutter in his hand.

Eagerly he found the catch to extend the blade, pushed it up a notch and tried to direct it into the ropes around his wrists. He managed to cut himself on the wrist. He realised he was still too wobbly so he turned around and leant over the desk to brace himself and managed to guide the blade into the ropes and start cutting them with a series of tiny sawing actions.

He was sure that he would be caught at any moment by the man who should have been there, Kenny presumably, but remarkably he did not get caught. He managed to free his hands and then his legs.

He sat down in the chair, massaging the rope chafed skin around his wrists and realised he still had more to do. Whatever was going on was not proper and he knew what he needed to do in that case, call the police.

Andy searched his pockets and discovered his phone was gone. No trouble. He opened the bottom cupboard on the right and pulled out the landline. Whoever had taken his phone was obviously not that observant. The telephone line that came to the booth was the only thing that wasn't road or nature as far as the eye could see.

Andy dialled emergency services and tried to explain what he thought was happening.

Chapter 30.

Maggie was used to going out on adventures with her Brother in law. She'd quickly learned to always come wearing shoes that you could move around in easily and that you didn't mind getting dirty. Her sneakers were white, admittedly, but good quality and she'd flown away from the man, getting a good lead and rounding the front of the ship and back to the pool area.

She knew she'd managed to get away quickly but she didn't know if she could keep that lead so as soon as she checked behind herself and couldn't see the man she ducked into a thick planter box containing shrubs, small trees and assorted greenery and dove into its centre, lying as flat and still as she could.

She could see, through the base of some plants, as the man puffed around the corner and took in the large expanse ahead of him. He slowed to a jog and then a walk and started surveying the area, looking for her. He looked hot, flustered and annoyed, a terrible combination in her opinion, and was muttering to himself angrily.

Mitchell surveyed the large pool area. Normally he would have kept running around the ship and heading for the exit but these kids had made him paranoid and he didn't want to be outsmarted again, he just wanted to tie up all these loose ends and get out of there. Unfortunately, the loose ends kept multiplying, escaping, running and getting looser.

In the planter box, Maggie realised that she needed to sneeze. She did not want to but a bead of something was running down the inside of her nose and try as she might she could feel the sneeze building up in her, reaching the point of no return.

As it came out she reached out, grabbed her nose, covered her mouse and tried to turn it into the smallest sneeze ever recorded in a human, but, sneezes being sneezes, the release had to come somewhere and whilst she contained most of it she could not stop herself from letting out a small squeak.

That was enough.

Mitch walked straight to the planter box, peeked in and stood back, arms folded. 'You! Out now.' He ordered.' Maggie did not move straight away. 'Now!' he screamed.

That did it, she climbed out, easing herself to the ground and standing in front of him, face to face. 'And Who. Are. You!' she exclaimed.

'None of your business, and don't take that tone with me. You with that other guy. You with Jack and kids?'

Maggie was surprised to hear Jack's name. 'Yes, yes I am.'

'Fine. Well, you can't be here, this is not safe. Come with me I'll take you to them and then you can all leave together when it's safe to do so. Understood.' Mitchell stood back and gestured with his arm the direction he wanted her to go.

'I'm not going anywhere with you until....' she began.

Mitchell clenched his jaw and interrupted her. 'Please, enough. You can't be on this ship, it's not safe. We'll help take you off when we're done but right now you can't be running around the ship. The rest of my maintenance crew needs to finish up their work okay?' he tried a smile, and almost succeeded.

'Let's see what the police have to say about his shall we?' said Maggie, pulling out her dead phone. It was a silly move. Mitchell's face dropped and he quickly snapped the phone out of her hand and put it in his pocket.

'I don't have time for this mucking about. Come with me now, we can do it easy or hard, either way I'm going to take you to the rest of them.' He grabbed her wrist and she resisted but, try as she might, she found the grip incredibly strong.

Sometime later, slowly, and with a lot of complaining from both Maggie and Mitchell, and hurt feelings all round, they came to the morgue.

Maggie saw the sign and started fighting again.

'For crying out loud, it's just where the kids are. I assume you want to see them.' said Mitchell, banging on the door. 'Hello in there, stand back from the door right now.'

'Okay' came Jack's voice through the door.

Mitchell made a *You See!* gesture with his free hand and then used it to untie the clumsily tied knot in the fire extinguisher hose and his swipe pass to open the door.

He pulled it open enough to push a person through, pushed Maggie through and quickly slammed the door again, tying the knot again with the hose.

'Who was that?' came a voice from behind him. It was Robbie, looking concerned.

'To be honest, I don't know and don't care. Hopefully she's the lot of them though. Far out, I was not expecting any of this. Anyhow, how you going?'

Robbie shrugged laconically. 'Almost done. One more load to get up to the entrance and then just need to finish cleaning the inside of the rooms to make sure we haven't left any evidence behind. Need maybe ten minutes.'

'Fine, you need my help?' asked Mitchell.

'I guess if you could make sure there's no more people walking around the bloomin' ship it would be good.'

Mitchell gave Robbie a very insincere smile. 'I'll do my best.' he said, walking down the corridor. 'Let me come help clear the room, then we can wait for you on the deck.'

'Sure.' shrugged Robbie. 'This has been a bit weird for my liking, not used to being with kids.'

'Ain't you got four?' asked Mitch.

Robbie shrugged again. 'I do. But they don't tend to be at my work.'

Chapter 31.

Isaac took his ear off the door and turned to the room. 'They're gone.' he said.

Maggie was walking around the room hugging everyone in turn and saved the last for Isaac who had shushed her and put his ear against the door as soon as it had closed.

It was nice to see her of course but they were somewhat confused as to why she was there, so she explained how she'd woken up feeling better and had wanted to see them.

She then pointed out, rather fairly, that her being there was definitely not the most confusing thing about their situation and so they explained what they knew so far and everything that had happened to them as quickly as possible.

'Did you see anyone in the booth?' asked Tabby. 'Was Jack's friend there.'

'I didn't see anyone in the booth no, it was empty but I didn't look in, I just drove through the open gate.'

Sandy sat on the floor and put her head in her hands. 'I hope he's okay.' She said. 'It's not fair that this has happened to him, I feel like it's our fault.'

'Don't be ridiculous.' said Jack. 'If they had known we were here they'd have never come at all. Whatever they're up to it's not our fault. However, I do agree, I am worried about Andy too. But I am more worried about all of us. Oh! Mags, I don't suppose you have a working phone on you do you?'

She shook her head. 'No. He took it off me and it was dead anyway.'

Over in the corner of the morgue, below the refrigerated metal doors, sitting on the floor Isaac and Tommo were having a quiet and very intense conversation. It was so quiet that the girls, Maggie and Jack did not even notice it at first but eventually the intensity of it caught their attention and one by one they turned to watch them as their conversation became a more heated whisper and eventually seemed to bloom into some sort of agreement or shared understanding.

The two boys turned back to see what the silence was about and found eight eyes looking directly at them.

'What's happening?' asked Tommo. 'Why are you all staring at us?'

Sandy laughed. 'Something caught our eye. Do you guys by any chance have a plan?'

The boys exchanged glances and nervous smiles before Isaac answered. 'I think we do.' He said, before walking to the door and looking through the crack.

He pointed up, 'Tommo noticed it, this room is shorter than the corridor, the ceiling is lower. That means there must be some space between the ceiling in here. I think we need to just push one of the ceiling panels up. We're getting out of here. This isn't right and we have to go for help.'

Jack and Maggie exchanged impressed glances, before nodding. 'What do you need?' asked Jack.

'Something to stand on. It looks like these panels here can move.' Isaac pointed right above him. 'But I don't think we can move any of the desks over. They're all stuck to the floor.'

'What about if you get on my shoulders, Isaac? You think you'll be steady enough?'

'Not really Dad.' he said. 'You haven't been able to lift me on your shoulders since I was seven.'

Maggie looked at the ceiling and then at Isaac, weighing the situation up. 'What about if I help support you too. We could form something like a pyramid.'

Tommo chimed in from across the room. 'There's no need, we can climb up. Look.' He was standing by the fridges that he knew were used to put people in. With a little fear, he pulled the lever and opened the first stainless steel door. He was relieved that it was not cold, that meant it was turned off which also meant there was definitely no people inside. He opened the next one up and climbed up on the first one to open the top one.

The room filled with a clear smell of disinfectant as Tom climbed to the top hole he had opened and reached up, grabbing a roof square and pushing it up. He managed to move it to one side then pulled himself up and through it using the top of the fridges as a ledge.

'What do you see?' asked Maggie.

'Not a lot. It's very dark. But I can see a little bit of light over by the wall. I think we can get out.'

'How much space is there?' asked Jack. 'From the ceiling to the... other ceiling.'

'I don't know. Maybe fifty centimetres. Hold on.'

They all watched the ceiling as Tommo's feet disappeared through the hole. One by one the tiles gave a little, bending down towards them. Jack moved underneath the moving ceiling tiles, ready to break the fall of Tom if he did fall through but the ceiling held.

When he reached the wall Tommo investigated the light source. It was a vent, not huge, but large enough for him to fit through he knew. In the dark, he felt around the edges of the vent and found some catches on each side on springs.

'What's happening?' called up Isaac.

'Hold on.' called back Tom, concentrating. He managed to force one of the catches up and push the vent out just a little and then repeated the feat with two more. The last one gave on its own and the vent fell to the corridor with a bang.

Everyone in the room turned to the door, not sure what to expect.

In the ceiling Tommo realised he could not go through head first and instead turned around and pushed his feet through the opening until they were dangling and he grabbed on to the edge, lowering himself and then letting go and dropping nimbly to the ground.

He walked to the door and knocked on it, untying the hose that was tied around the handles. 'I'm out.' he said distractedly. 'But I don't know what to do with the door. There was something tied on it, which I've taken off, but I don't know how I can open it.'

Isaac laughed. 'You don't need to. We can follow you.'

'Will we all fit?' asked Jack.

'I don't know.' said Tommo. 'But try, and quickly, please. Feet first.' He stepped back and looked at the hole in the wall again before calling through the door again. 'I think Mum will fit at least.'

Jack didn't stop to mention that he was barely larger than Maggie himself, even if he was not as slim as in his youth. He repeated his monitoring of the tiles as first the girls, then Isaac and finally Maggie climbed up through the hole and dropped down into the corridor, each of them coming through before the next one started.

Finally, it was Jack's turn. He pulled himself up the pleasantly clean fridges and into the ceiling cavity. It was, he knew, without needing to look, and based only on the smell, filthy. No one had ever cleaned up here, why would they. Every crawling step he made, spreading his weight as wide as possible across the ceiling panels, he felt the dirt on his palms and being pressed into the knees of his trousers.

In reality, it took him just twenty or so seconds to make his way through the void but it felt like a hellish eternity. When he came to the opening he didn't stop to check if he would fit, nor to turn around, he just launched himself through headfirst, desperate to escape the dirt.

He landed on the floor with a loud bump, landing on his head, quite unconscious.

Chapter 32.

Maggie checked Jack's pulse and breathing and seemed satisfied that he was merely knocked out and nothing more serious. 'He'll need to see a doctor at some point.' she said. 'But right now I don't know what to do with him.'

'We need to move him.' insisted Tabby. 'Otherwise, when the men come back he could be in danger.'

'I think I know where they are.' said Isaac. 'I could hear them. I'm tired of running away from them and trying to hide and getting trapped. I think we should trap them.'

'We can't do that.' Maggie said. 'It's too dangerous.'

Isaac appeared insulted by this suggestion. 'I don't think so. One of them is downstairs, in the safe room. He said he was going to be in the safe itself. Well if he still is we can lock him in there. And the other two, they're so stupid I think we can trap them somewhere too. Look, all day they've been catching us and we've escaped. I bet they can't.'

'I agree.' said Sandy. 'I'm worried about Uncle Jack, I'm worried about Andy, we need to get out of here and we need to make sure these guys don't. This isn't right. People shouldn't be allowed to just come on board and do what they like, locking people up and all sorts.'

'I can't let you do anything dangerous.' said Maggie calmly. 'We should find a quiet place where we can see them leave. I'm not sure about moving Jack, but we probably should. It's a shame we're not back in there, we could have used one of those gurneys...'

Maggie was cut short speaking. Isaac had darted off down the corridor. The other kids looked at her and then followed. Maggie called at them to stop but they ignored her. She looked down at Jack, wished him luck in her head and trotted off after the kids.

She was familiar with the determination of Lisa and Jack's kids. She had grown up with a version of it in her own house with her sister always being so sure headed and determined when there was something she believed in. If she couldn't stop them, she could certainly help them.

They came to the staircase and Isaac peaked around and listened intently then struck off across it and headed down to the next level, turning left and heading towards the safe room, slowing to a tip-toe as he got close to the door.

The other kids caught up behind him, and then Maggie, but he turned and shushed them, looking so certain of himself that they instantly obeyed and watched. Isaac poked his head around the open doors and looked inside. The room was empty but the door to the safe room was open. He could hear someone in there doing... something.

He surveyed the room and saw just a small bag left in the room and on the floor next to it a passkey. That was exactly what he had hoped for. He crept into the room, ignoring the quiet pleas from Maggie to stop and came to the safe door, standing behind it.

Robbie had his back to him inside the room, which was filled on each wall with black metal doors of different sizes. Robbie was using a spray bottle and some wipes and seemed to be spot cleaning the floor. This was too easy. Isaac looked at the door, realised it was too heavy for him to close quickly so he turned back to the door and pointed at the kids' faces behind it, indicating for them to sneak in quietly, using his fingers to mime out tip-toeing.

The kids all came to the door with him and followed his instructions to put their hands on it. He held up one hand and counted down... three... two... one... and then put the hand on the door.

Altogether they shifted the massive weight of the door and slammed it shut. Robbie noticed the light changing and looked up, but didn't even have time to move before it slammed shut. He quickly started searching his pockets for his pass and remembered exactly where he'd left it.

Robbie punched the wall in anger, hurting his hand. 'Bloody Terry Brothers!' he screamed in anger. He started banging on the thick metal, padded, well-insulated security door.

Outside the safe no one heard him. Isaac grabbed the bag of things and the pass. 'Come on.' He said. 'We know they'll come back looking for him, let's get out of here make it look he's already gone.'

'No.' said Tabby. 'We need them to follow us right? How else are we going to catch them.'

Sandy joined in. 'She's right. Let's leave them a trail of breadcrumbs. Come on.' She grabbed the bag and started looking inside it. There was a variety of tools, bags, bits and pieces of plastic, fasteners.

She took out a spanner and left it on the floor of the corridor outside the room and started running off down the hallway. 'Follow me.' she called.' But they already were.

Chapter 33.

Blake and Terry had been waiting on the gantry for Robbie to finish up and come join them for some time.

'You think we should take it to the van?' asked Blake.

'No, I think we should stay here and make sure it's all finished.' snapped Mitchell

'We could come back after. Seems silly just standing here with all these bags.'

'Sure. We could take it, but we can't take it all, so if Robbie doesn't come straight behind us we'll have to come straight back here and wait. And what happens if he then does come back and says... *Almost done just need to...* I don't know what he'd need to, but it would require something from one of these bags. Then we'd have to go all the way to the van again, get it, come back here, wait some more and then go back again.'

'So you think we should just wait here?' asked Blake.

'Yes.' Mitchell replied. 'Well... no maybe not.' He checked his watch and then looked out at the sky. It was late afternoon now, still light but getting late. They didn't know at what point the man in the booth would be missed but they didn't want to be there longer than they had to. 'Come on' he said. 'Let's go get Robbie, help him finish up and then get the hell off this boat.'

'Sure thing brother.' said Blake, following him on the well-worn route down to the insides of the ship.

They walked in silence, not the comfortable silence of siblings but the annoyed silence of two people doing things they didn't want to be doing but had to. That was true for Mitchell anyway, Blake was happy enough to be keeping busy. He didn't like just standing around and Mitchell often made him do it.

They came down to the floor with the safe room and saw the doors closed. Mitchell opened them with his pass and found the entire room deserted. Robbie must have left.

'Look.' Blake said from behind him. He turned and saw what he was pointing at. There was a spanner on the floor.

Mitchell picked it up and put it in his pocket when something caught his eye further down the corridor, a small pile of wall plugs.

They went to those and put them in a pocket too and continued down the corridor. Every ten to twenty feet they found something they had to pick up and stow in an increasingly full pocket.

'I don't like this.' Mitchell muttered.

Blake shrugged. 'I think Robbie left us a trail to follow.'

'Maybe, but he knows we can't leave this stuff here, it's probably covered in fingerprints and who knows what.'

'Why else would he have left them though? Maybe he needs help.'

'Maybe, or maybe he's got a hole in his bag and doesn't realise it. Or maybe it's those bloody kids.'

'You want me to go check on them?'

'No. We need to find Robbie and get the hell out of here no matter what. I don't care about those kids or that man or the woman, none of it, we get out, we slash their tyres and we keep going until we're as far away as possible.' He stooped to collect a packet of tissues from the floor, handing it to Blake to carry.

They came to a door leading into the ship that was held open a crack by a screwdriver. They followed the corridor it led to across the ship and to a staircase that led them upstairs with a packet of screws and then some lip balm.

At the top of the stairs, they found another door held open with a screwdriver and came out on to the walkway on the opposite side of the ship to the gantry. They looked both ways and couldn't see any more stuff to find.

'Where they go?' asked Blake.

'Shhh.' grunted Mitchell. Something had caught his eye to his right, something out of place. There was a large planter box filled with soil and greenery every twenty or so feet along the corridor and one about four boxes down from them had something just poking out from behind it.

Who's the seeker now! Thought Mitchell as he started running towards the box in question.

At the sound of his heavy footfalls, Tom emerged and started running at full pelt.

'This again! Come on Blake!' screamed Mitchell as he ran, Blake following.

The boy disappeared around the curve of the ship but he had not been as fast as he thought he was. As Mitchell came round the bend he clearly saw a foot disappearing into a lifeboat hanging out over the railing.

Gotcha thought Mitchell, coming to the boat and diving into it through the same opening in the material he had seen the foot disappear into. He found himself in a crowded lifeboat with containers of various sorts, all covered by a heavy tarpaulin that was connected to the rim of the boat by heavy elastic cords.

Blake piled in after Mitchell, landing on his brother's legs and sending Mitchell sprawling on the floor in the middle of the boat.

From behind a pile of life jackets, the boy emerged, smirked and then jumped out of the boat at the other end through an opening in the tarpaulin covering.

'Get out!' shouted Mitchell, trying to first get himself out from under Blake, when the world started moving weirdly.

From their hiding places, the three kids and Maggie had appeared and engaged the emergency release on the lifeboat which was now being lowered down into the void between the ship and the side of the dock.

By the time Mitchell managed to get his head out of the boat and look up they were too far gone to get back on the boat and getting further from it by the second. Blake popped his head out too and saw the kids and the lady waving at them from the deck. Despite himself, he waved back.

'Idiots.' said Mitchell.

'Don't be hard on yourself.' Blake countered.

'Not us, them. They think they got us, but when we get to the bottom we can just get out and climb out again. This isn't over.'

Mitchell's thoughts on this matter lasted another fifteen or so seconds, seconds he spent scowling at the kids. That was as long as it took for the ropes that lowered the boat to reach the end of their runoff. The boat, after all, was designed to lower down to the water, not to the bottom of the keel.

The winching mechanism ground to a halt, the boat stopped and sat suspended in the air, swaying gently in the breeze. It was, in fact, over.

From the deck, the kids and Maggie heard the gnashing screams but walked away. It was not language suitable for children so young.

Chapter 34.

The police crew arrived, two cars containing two officers each and followed shortly after by an ambulance.

Andy met them at the open gate and tried to relay what had happened and what they needed to do but was having trouble explaining it.

Eventually, he made himself understood. 'There's someone here up to no good. They came in that van so they must still be here but one of them took my car.'

'Okay.' said the officer. 'So you're reporting a stolen car?'

'No, I'm reporting... there are people that need help. A family. Jack and four kids. They're on the ship and so is someone else, someone who knocked me out. I don't know what they're doing but they shouldn't be here.'

The officer talked to his colleagues and left one with Andy to try and get some more sense out of him whilst the medics started examining him and making sure he was okay. They shone lights in his eyes, told him he was concussed and put a bandage around his head since he had some cuts on the back where he'd been donked.

The other officers drove down to the stairs leading up to the gantry and got out.

The first officer, Jane Teal, was the most senior officer and tried to explain what was happening to the other two.

'It's a bit vague.' she said. 'Someone hit him so he might be talking nonsense about some of this but it sounds like there are some people trespassing on the ship that we need to find, maybe some others too, more like visitors. He seemed concerned about their safety. I called the station just now and asked them to get in contact with the private security company that works this site, and the site owners, so hopefully we'll get a bit of help. For now I suggest we head up there and see what we can. One way in and out, straight up.' She pointed up.

The three officers made their way up the stairs and across the gantry to the ship. On the walkway they came across a collection of bags, some of them bulky. Officer Teal bent down and looked in one of the bags, opening it carefully. She found a blow torch staring out at her.

'Looks like tools of the trade alright.' said the youngest officer, Dennis Field.

'Agreed.' said Officer Teal surveying the deck in each direction whilst Officer Field called it in. This was a crime scene clearly and they'd need a scene crew to come in and start photographing and recording what they were finding. 'What you reckon?' she continued, talking to her other colleague, Officer Dale, a short and experienced officer with wispy grey hair.

'I don't know'. He said. 'I'm not sure where to start. I would guess we need some more hands and create a perimeter.'

'It's massive though.' said Officer Teal, taking off her hat and then securing it back on her head more firmly. 'Top down, back to front, floor by floor. I guess we should probably try and work out why they'd be here at all. Start there...'

She was interrupted by a coo-ee from along the deck. All three officers turned to the noise. Despite having been warned about a man and four kids somehow actually seeing them coming towards them was a surprise, as was a lady of whom there'd been no mention, supporting him on her shoulder.

The kids started running and came up to them before the adults, all talking at once.

The three officers could only get wisps of the story, coming at them from all direction.

'They locked us up...'

'In the lifeboat...'

'...Then a morgue...'

'We left them breadcrumbs...'

'Trapped in the safe...'

'... hide and seek.'

But the chatter slowly coalesced to a single question as the adults arrived behind the children.

'Is Andy okay?' asked Tabby. 'Did you see him?'

Officer Teal zeroed in on that clarity. 'The gentleman who runs the booth?' The kids nodded and affirmed. 'Think he's got a bit of a sore head but is otherwise okay. I was not sure he was making much sense talking about a bunch of kids here but I guess he was. I take it you're Jack?' she asked.

'Indeed. I'm Jack, this is Maggie,' he gestured to her, 'and these are Isaac, Tom, Tabby and Sandy.'

Officer Dale chipped in. 'And what exactly are you all doing here?'

'A good question' answered Jack. 'You don't mind if I sit down do you? I've a rather sore head.' Jack leant against a wall and slid down to sit against it.

'Have you been hurt sir?' asked Officer Field.

'I have. My own doing really but my head is quite sore. I wouldn't mind a lie down. In fact...' he lay down.

Officer Field called the paramedics and asked for some assistance whilst Officers Teal and Dale took the kids and Maggie to one side and asked them a series of pointed questions to try and understand what had happened.

They learnt about the three men on board. They also learnt about their current locations. Officer Oldfield even trotted around the ship to check on the lifeboat and came back confirming the story.

They also learned about the other man, locked in the safe, and Isaac offered them the pass he'd taken. 'I can take you to him if you like?' he said.

Officer Teal shook her head and smiled. 'No that's okay. It sounds like you've done enough for one day. We might just wait for some of our colleagues to come and join us and we'll go visit him ourselves. Do you think you can give me directions?'

Isaac nodded and explained where the safe room was whilst the officers took notes in their pads.

'I think,' said Officer Teal, 'That it might be best now if you left the ship. Do you think you could go back to the booth and wait there? We'll have some more questions, but I think we can take it from here.'

'What about my dad?' asked Tabby. 'Can he come with us?'

'Sure can. Just let the medics have a quick look at him first. They should be on their way up.'

Sandy went to the side of the boat and looked down. She could see two new police cars arriving down the road, as well as a police van, and a second ambulance. She pointed them out to the other kids and they watched as they pulled up down below.

Officer Dale took them and Maggie and led them down the stairs, past the waiting officers and walked with them to the booth. A short while later Jack was helped off the crime scene, walked with assistance down the stairs and was put into the back of the ambulance there.

The kids waited and watched as more people arrived. Security staff and management people. Then more police cars and finally a news van, then another, journalists too. A helicopter started circling overhead as the sun began to go down.

As night took over lights set into the dry dock were turned on, casting the Radiant Queen a bright silhouette of beautiful colourful cruise ship against the black sky.

Chapter 35.

Jack had to stay in the local hospital overnight, just to keep an eye on him and he'd ended up sharing a room with Andy who was similarly sore of head.

They had both been firmly questioned by various policeman over the course of the night and Jack suspected that one or both of them was somehow suspected of being involved with the criminal activity but as the night wore on the tone of the questions changed dramatically and it seemed clear enough that whatever suspicion there had been had now disappeared.

The next day he was released and cleared to drive and was driven to the police station where his car had been taken. It was a long and boring drive on his own, but he made sure he stopped regularly and rested, recuperated, took painkillers.

More than anything he wanted to get back to his kids.

They had all driven home late the previous night he'd been told. His phone, like Maggie's, was still held as evidence and when he'd tried to call them from the police station to Maggie's house it had rung out and not been answered.

He arrived at the Myer-Stone residence a little after one in the afternoon and was greeted as he pulled up by four happy faces at the lounge room window. He jumped out of the car and hadn't yet made it to the door when it was flung open and his kids were on him, hugging the life out of him. A few moments later his niece and nephew were there too.

Maggie stood in the doorway and when the kids had let him free beckoned Jack over and gave him a warm hug too. 'Just in time.' she said. 'We all slept in so we're just about to have a bit of a late brunch.'

'My favourite!' said Jack. 'Need me to whip up some eggs.'

'It's all done.' said Maggie. 'You're the guest of honour, our wounded soldier, you don't have to do a thing. Come on kids. Wash up. Brunch is served.'

The kids all cleaned their hands in one bathroom while Jack used the small sink in the laundry and then they joined Jack at the round table in the kitchen table.

Maggie had gone all out. There was fresh fruit, cut up and arranged on a plate in colour order. There was muesli and yogurt and frozen berries to create your own bircher bowl. There were bacon, eggs and some sausages ('From frozen I'm afraid.' Maggie had apologised.)

There was toast, and it kept coming, as well as butter, jams, peanut butter, vegemite, homemade cumquat marmalade, a bowl of baked beans, a bowl of avocados and, of course, a steaming hot pot of tea right in the middle.

Jack discovered, in a very, very quick instant, that he was absolutely ravenous and didn't know even where to start. The kids meanwhile took the opposite approach of starting with everything, piling up their plates with every yummy thing they could. Maggie saw the hesitation on Jack's face and started putting food on his plate.

It was all good, so he was happy with everything he had on his plate and started consuming it with a passion.

'We had McDonald's last night.' Tommo told him. 'We stopped on the way home and ate it in the car.'

Maggie shrugged. 'Only place open.'

'Happy meal?' asked Jack.

'I'm too old for Happy meals.' Tommo told him.

'I'm not.' said Isaac, two years Tom's senior. 'I had a happy meal. I got a toy Pokémon.'

'Yeah.' said Tommo. 'I wish I'd got one too.'

Jack sighed. 'Well, this is my happy meal. I can't tell you how nice it is to be here with you all. It was a weird night alright. Andy and I must have been terrible company for the nurses, both a bit delirious and saying odd things to the nurses like how we'd only been having an epic game of hide and seek and that the head injury was caused by escaping from a morgue.'

Everyone laughed.

'Was Andy okay then?' asked Isaac.

'Yes, I think so. He might be in a bit of trouble at work but since he technically... you know... saved the day, I think he'll be alright.'

'Oh! We saw us on the internet.' said Tabby. 'Well not us,

but the ship. They had a whole news article about it. They said it was a... what was it?' she asked Sandy.

'They said it was a *Grand Theft Cruiseship*. I don't really understand it but they said it was a... an incident on the ship and they mentioned us. All of us. They said it was a plot that was foiled by a family that happened to be on board. That's us! We're the family.'

'Oh gosh.' said Maggie. 'And some of those reporters were asking a lot of questions but all of you did very well doing what the police officer said and saying nothing. You are witnesses after all.'

Jack hooted and smacked the table. 'Witnesses to the most exciting game of hide and seek there's ever been!'

Maggie sniggered. 'That too. Although I wouldn't like to think this would become a regular sort of thing.'

Sandy hooted herself. 'Come on Mum! Those guys were amateurs compared with us. I still can't believe they fell for the trap on the lifeboat.'

'I can't believe you thought of it!' said Maggie.

Sandy looked a little embarrassed. 'I didn't really. That's what Tommo used to do all the time when we were playing back to base. He'd run in a cubby house then jump out the window and you'd be stuck in there and he'd get away.'

Maggie sat backed and watched her family attacking their brunch with gusto. She was so glad they were all okay she didn't even know where to put the emotion. But the ghastly absence of her sister was there in the room too. She felt a tear come to her eye and tried to stop it coming out but couldn't, and they started flowing down her cheek.

Tommo put his hand on her arm. 'Don't cry Mum.' he said. 'We're all okay.'

'I know.' Maggie replied. 'It's not that. It's just seeing you all here, and seeing you all yesterday, and you were all so brave, and so resilient, and so determined to do the right thing and not let those men get away with whatever they were trying to do. It's just... Lisa would have been so proud, of all of you, and to see you here all so happy, it makes me miss her. But I guess... I really should be happy that we've all got each other.

From across the table, Maggie's words moved Jack deeply. He was started crying too, but tears of happiness and an outpouring of emotion from the previous twenty-four hours. The kids looked at them both, smirked at each other and went back to their brunch quietly.

Maggie pulled a hankie out of her sleeve, passed one to Jack and kept one for herself.

Chapter 36.

As Sam Myer-Stone came through the checkpoint at the airport he scanned the assembled people looking for his little family. He couldn't see them anywhere but didn't want to hold up the other passengers so he kept walking passed the magic line that told you that you had made it home, moved off to one side and put his trolley against a wall.

He pulled out his phone to check for messages but there was none. They were either running late or had got the timings wrong. He started dialling his wife when suddenly six hands appeared around him as if from nowhere, his kids and wife hugging him tightly.

They embraced and then he stood back and looked at them all.

'Tom, I believe you have grown exactly naught point four centimetres since I saw you last. And Sandy, you have not grown. But! Your hair has, by almost one inch, which seems impossible. And finally my beautiful wife. I would tell you that you had become even more beautiful except you would know I was lying because you were already perfect.'

'Stop it!' said Maggie, although she certainly did not mind the compliments. 'How was your trip?'

'It was fine. It was work. Exciting, fun and interesting but still work. However, I did not manage to foil a single robbery or have any of the sort of adventures you guys seem to have had.'

'Foil?' asked Tommo.

'It's a good job Jack isn't here either.' said Sam. 'I think I should strangle him for getting you into this pickle, but then hug him for getting you all out again.'

'Oh he didn't get us out.' laughed Maggie. 'He knocked himself out jumping through a vent and lay on the floor whilst these kids took care of the bad guys. But we can fill you in later, let's go home, we still have a week of summer holiday, let's go enjoy them.

In the car on the way back to their house, Sandy and Tom filled their father in on all the adventurous details of their encounters. They told him all about the boat and its different areas, as well as their games of hide and seek, their various captures and escapes and how they'd finally managed to get one over on all the bad men.

They also told him about their various dealings with the police giving evidence, and how eventually the criminals had all pleaded guilty. Between the bits and pieces that Isaac and the rest had overheard and picked up, combined with the tools and the plans the police had found on the ship, it was enough to complete a very convincing case as to exactly what they had been planning to do on that ship, and the three men had not only given themselves up but had also brought another man in as well, the one that had fled the scene at the first sign of trouble.

'And by trouble Dad, just so you understand, that means us.' bragged Tommo.

'I'm sure!' said Sam. 'I don't know if I am sad to have missed it or glad to have avoided it!'

They got home and the kids rushed off as Sam sat at the kitchen table, holding his wife's hand and smiling at her whilst the kettle boiled. Their peace lasted a few seconds.

Sandy and Tommo ran in with their folder of news articles, print outs and official documents that they'd compiled of their adventure. On the front page was them, standing with the police chief and their cousins, receiving bravery badges for their work. Excitedly they took him through all of it and he patiently listened. More than patiently. He was amazed, proud and fascinated.

Chapter 37.

Summer ended as all summers do and the kids went back to school. As autumn rolled in and the leaves changed, the birds left or came, the winds roared across the fields and Maggie was back on her canvasses, chronicling what she saw in her own unique style.

During school terms it was harder to see Jack and his kids regularly, the distance between them was too far to just pop over, and weekends were often filled with sports, activities and friends. They'd been talk of another hide and seekers expedition but so far it had not happened.

Sam had returned to the university and was teaching again, and enjoying it as he always did. As he said, it was not the teaching he enjoyed, but the meeting new engaged students, for no one studied archaeology who did not want to and Sam's stories from the field were always a firm hit.

Autumn started creeping towards winter and the first of the colds began. Sensible jumpers and coats came out of the attic and the days became slower and more internal.

The Myer-Stone kids had been minor celebrities at school when they'd gone back but they'd not shown off or carried on so things were quickly back to normal.

It was almost, but not quite, getting a little boring.

One day, a few weeks before the break for the Winter school holidays, Sam came rushing to the dinner table with a spring in his step.

'Great news!' he said, sitting down. 'Do you remember I was in Uzbekistan in the summer? Well when I was there I met this lady called Leona Bridges, she's... sort of a big deal... she funds a lot of digs through her foundation. Anyway, evidentially I made an impression because I just spoke to the director of their foundation and they offered me a job, just a month or so, over the break.'

'Dad!' said Tommo. 'I thought you were going to be here now.'

'Let me finish!' snapped Sam happily. 'I haven't got to the best part. I said that I didn't want to leave you all, and they said that they really wanted me and that I could bring you all with. You can come with and they'll put us all up in a house near the site.'

'Where?' asked Maggie and Sandy at the same time.

'Wait, that's still not the best bit. Then I said that even if all of you came, I would feel terrible leaving my brother-in-law and my niece and nephew behind and they said the house that they have near the site is big enough for all of us and everyone could come.'

'They must really want you!' said Maggie.

'Or they just don't know what they're letting themselves in for.' Sam replied. 'Either way, what do you guys think? Do you want to come? I know Jack will.'

'Where!' said Sandy, Maggie and Tom all in unison.

'Oh, didn't I mention that. Sam laughed. 'It's in the Valdivian rainforest in Chile. They call it the rainforest at the end of the world! They found the ruins of a temple and need someone who knows what they're doing to lead the dig.'

Join us next time for....

The Hide and Seekers and the Temple of Truth

That's it.

The book's over.

Why are you still reading it?

Adoni Patrikios is a writer based in Sydney in Australia.

He lives in a castle made of cheese and eats new rooms for himself most days.

Made in United States
North Haven, CT
30 June 2022

20796792R00140